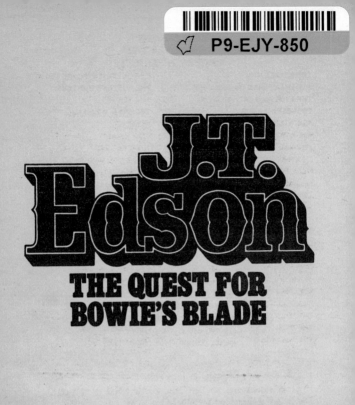

J.T. Edson

THE QUEST FOR BOWIE'S BLADE

CHARTER BOOKS, NEW YORK

This Charter book contains the complete
text of the original hardcover edition.
It has been completely reset in a typeface
designed for easy reading and was printed
from new film.

THE QUEST FOR BOWIE'S BLADE

A Charter Book / published by arrangement with
Transworld Publishers, Ltd.

PRINTING HISTORY
Corgi edition published 1974
Berkley edition / November 1982
Charter edition / November 1988

ISBN: 1-55773-143-8

Charter Books are published by The Berkley Publishing Group,
200 Madison Avenue, New York, NY 10016.
The name "CHARTER" and the "C" logo are
trademarks belonging to Charter Communications, Inc.

PRINTED IN THE UNITED STATES OF AMERICA

10 9 8 7 6 5 4 3 2 1

For Douglas "The Red Baron" and
Anne "Injun-Lover" Revell

AUTHOR'S NOTE:

Once again, to avoid repetition for my regular readers, the histories of the floating outfit and Belle Boyd are given in the form of appendices.

The dimensions of James Bowie's knife are those of William Randall Junior's Model 12 "Smithsonian Bowie Knife" which is an identical copy of the original.

THE QUEST FOR
BOWIE'S BLADE

CHAPTER ONE

Give Me *The* Knife

From the plaza came a rising cacophony of shouts, shots, the clashing of steel against steel, all intermingled with screams of men in mortal agony. They told a grim story to the two occupants of the room in the hospital.

Clearly at last, on March 6th, 1836, the defenses of the Franciscan Order's disused *Mission San Antonio de Valera*—which was more frequently referred to as the "Alamo" Mission on account of it once having been surrounded by a grove of *alamo*, cottonwood trees—had been breached. Although as yet it had not reached the hospital building, a savage, bloody hand-to-hand, no-quarter conflict was raging on the plaza and in the convent. The bitterness of the fighting was, in part, caused by memories of the events which had preceded it.

For the past thirteen days, one hundred and eighty-three men under the joint command of Colonels William Barrett Travis, Davey Crockett and James Bowie—although the latter was bedridden with a broken leg sustained in an accident while

1

helping to mount a cannon on the parapet—had contrived to
hold the Alamo Mission against a Mexican army which had
grown until it was over four thousand strong. By making their
stand in what had always been as much of a fort as a place of
worship, the small band of defenders were hoping to gain
sufficient time for Major General Samuel Houston to gather
together a force which would be strong enough to liberate the
newly created Republic of Texas from the tyrannical clutches
of the Mexican dictator, *Presidente* Antonio Lopez de Santa
Anna.

Right from the beginning, Travis and his commanders had
been realistic enough to admit there could be only one ending
to their efforts in spite of the heavy casualties which they were
inflicting upon their assailants. Long before a relief column
could arrive, even if Houston had had one to dispatch, Santa
Anna and his second-in-command, General Cos, would have
assembled enough men to launch such a massive assault that
the garrison—which had also suffered losses, if on a much
smaller scale, during the fighting—would be swamped under
by sheer weight of numbers. Once that happened, there would
be little or no hope of survival for any of the defenders. They
had been left with no doubts on that point.

Soon after his arrival on the scene, being desirous of bringing the seige to an end without further loss of life among his
army and wishing to avoid being delayed in his pursuit of
Houston, Santa Anna had instructed General Cos to present the
men inside the Alamo Mission with an opportunity to lay down
their arms and leave. Travis, Crockett and Bowie had guessed
what had motivated the offer and had realized that, by continuing their resistance, they might improve the Republic of
Texas's chances of throwing off the yoke of tyranny and oppres-
sion. What was more, they had doubted whether the Mexicans
would honor the terms of the capitulation.[1] In view of what
had happened a few months earlier, they had not regarded

1. Although the defenders of the Alamo Mission would not live to hear of
it, their distrust was well founded if a later incident was anything to go by.
When Colonel Fannin and four hundred men surrendered to a vastly superior
number of Mexicans at Goliad on March 27th, 1836, General Urrea—possibly
without Santa Anna's knowledge—ordered that they all were shot. Only twenty-
seven of the Texians—as the American born citizens of Texas called themselves
at that period—survived the massacre.

Cos's word of honor as being a satisfactory guarantee of their safety.[2] Nor had the despotic *Presidente* Santa Anna ever been noted for his compassion or mercy towards those who opposed him. So, after having had the situation explained to them, the defenders had elected to carry on with the fight. A warning that they would be granted no quarter if they did not accept Cos's offer had served to stiffen their resolve rather than sway them from their purpose.

Such was Santa Anna's rage over the defenders' defiance in the face of his ultimatum, the reply having been deliberately phrased in insulting terms so that it might produce the required reaction, that he had allowed it to cloud his judgement. Ignoring the advice of his senior officers, he had refused to follow what would have been the most sensible line of action. Instead of leaving a small force to contain the occupants of the Alamo Mission until starvation had driven them out, while he followed Houston with the rest of his army, he had sworn that he would not move on as long as one of the defenders remained alive.

There had been several attempts at dislodging the garrison during the days which had followed their refusal to surrender. Made for the most part by the poorly armed, badly trained Militia regiments—comprised of *peons* who had little desire to fight, but who had nevertheless been forced into Santa Anna's service—they were not carried out with any great resolution, and each had been repulsed.

However, with each succeeding day, the size of the Mexican army around the Alamo Mission had continued to increase in numbers. In his anger, Santa Anna had insisted upon calling on the services of two other columns which could have been put to a much more effective use elsewhere. By doing so, he had fallen into the trap which Travis, Bowie and Crockett had laid for him.

From the walls, the defenders had watched the preparations being made for a major assault. Scaling ladders had been manufactured in large numbers and brought forward. Batteries of

2. On December 10th, 1835, General Cos and his entire force of eleven hundred Mexican soldiers had surrendered to the Texians at San Antonio de Bexar. All had been released on giving their parole that they would take no further part in the fighting. Cos had gone back on his word and resumed hostilities almost immediately.

cannon had been assembled and sited. Lastly—and most significant—a vast pile of wood had been collected to be used as their funeral pyre. Obviously, *el Presidente* had been determined to crush their resistance no matter what the cost to his own men.

Although the price in dead and wounded had been high, the mass of Mexicans who had swarmed forward from every side would not stop. When the defenders' positions on the parapets had become untenable they had fallen back. Now the walls had been breached, they were continuing to sell their lives as dearly as possible.

Sitting on the bed in his hospital room, with his left leg held rigid by the splints which secured it, James Bowie knew that the end was drawing near. Not five minutes ago, having been sent to take care of Captain Dickinson's wife and daughter, Travis's Negro servant, Joe, had arrived to say that his master had been shot and killed on the northern wall. However, Dickinson and his men were still fighting. So, according to Joe, were Davey Crockett's Kentuckians and Bowie's own Texas Volunteers. For all that, Bowie realized, it was only a matter of time before it was all over.

A big man, well over six foot in height and broad with it, Bowie was still hard-muscled, strong and powerful despite his grey hair. Accepting that he was going to be killed, he was determined to go out fighting. There were two cocked pistols on the chair at the right of the bed and a big knife was sheathed on the belt which was hanging over its back.

"Get me on my feet, Sam," Bowie ordered, as the sounds of the fighting grew nearer. "I'm damned if I'll let them kill me lying on a bed."

"Sure thing, Mister Jim," the tall, well-made, white-haired Negro replied, setting down the double-barrelled shotgun which he had been holding as he stood by the window and reported on the progress of the battle.

Hurrying across the room, Sam helped his master to rise. Bowie grunted as, in spite of the Negro's assistance, pain shot through his broken leg. However, he braced his back against the wall and allowed Sam to slip a crutch under his left arm. While that took most of the strain from the injured limb, Bowie knew he would be unable to move from his position.

"That's better," Bowie gritted. "Now give me *the* knive."

There was an expression of reverence almost on the old Negro's face as he slid the knife from its sheath and handed it to his master. He knew what the great weapon meant to Bowie.

Closing his fingers around the concave ivory handle, specially made to suit his massive hand, Bowie flipped the sheath on to the bed. There was just the trace of a smile on his lined, tanned face as he looked at the great knife and felt the perfect way in which its forty-three-ounce weight balanced in his grasp. Razor sharp, the clip-pointed blade was eleven inches long, two and a quarter inches broad and three-eighths of an inch thick where it joined the brass-lugged hilt. James Black, the blacksmith and master cutler from Arkansas, had never produced a finer piece of work. While the knife had been made to an original design which Bowie had devised, it was Black who had turned it into more than just a superlative weapon. It was, in fact, unique.

So unique that Bowie wondered if he should have tried to send the knife and a letter of explanation to his friend Sam Houston. Unfortunately, as the siege had progressed, no man could have been spared from the ever-decreasing garrison. That was a pity, for the knife carried a clue which could make the fortune of anybody who knew its secret and could exploit it.

There was, Bowie realized, no time to spare for futile regrets over the lack of an opportunity to pass on his information. Probably James Black would be able to find some other way to attain the goal towards which they had been working. Bowie hoped so, remembering the number of times that the great knife created by the other's skilled workmanship had saved his life.

Thrusting all such reverie from his head, Bowie swung his gaze towards the pistols which Sam was holding. He spiked the point of the knife, with its cutting edge upwards, into the adobe wall alongside his left ear so it would be readily available when it was needed. Then, nodding his gratitude, he grasped the butts of the pistols.

Hearing approaching footsteps, Sam hurried across the room. Even as he was snatching up the shotgun, there was a crash and the door burst open. Before Sam could turn, he saw several men coming towards the window. Armed with old flintlock rifles and bayonets of the long, spiked variety, they wore straw *sombreros*, ragged white shirts and trousers, white leather cross-belts, red sashes and had home-made sandals on their feet. That meant they were soldiers of the Mexican Militia and not *Chicano*[3] members of the Texas Volunteers arriving to try to defend their colonel.

Facing inwards and holding their weapons in what bayonet fighters called the "high port" position, two more of the Militiamen entered the room. From all appearances, they had been expecting considerable resistance as they had shoulder-charged at the door and were taken by surprise when it had yielded very easily. However, they were not allowed to recover their equilibrium.

Bowie's right-hand pistol bellowed, vomiting smoke and propelling its heavy ball into the center of the taller man's forehead. As he spun in a half circle, dropping his rifle and clawing spasmodically at the wound, the big Texian's second weapon hurled death just as surely at his companion. With the lead tearing open his heart, the stricken Mexican was twirled around to blunder a few helpless steps before sprawling face down on the floor.

Already the next attacker was coming through the door, and one glance warned Bowie that he was likely to prove a much tougher proposition than the *peons* who formed the unwilling rank and file of the Militia. Big, burly, hard-faced, he had on a better-quality version of the previous pair's "uniform", with three stripes on the sleeves of the shirt and his trousers tucked into boots. What was more, unlike his predecessors, he was in control of his movements and held his rifle and bayonet ready for use.

Glaring at Bowie, the sergeant started to raise his weapon. At that moment, Sam's shotgun thundered and one barrel's charge of buckshot slashed through the window to tumble two of the approaching men as limp as rag dolls to the ground. Instantly, the sergeant swung his attention from the big Texian.

Deciding that the old Negro might pose a greater and more immediate danger than the crippled *gringo,* who was dropping what were obviously empty pistols, the sergeant acted to counter it. Swivelling at the hips, he whipped the butt of his

3. *Chicano:* Mexican-born citizen of Texas.

rifle to his shoulder and took aim.

"Look out, Sam!" Bowie roared, reaching up and across towards the hilt of his knife.

The warning came too late.

Lining his sights, the sergeant squeezed the trigger. From the fully cocked position, the simple mechanism propelled the flint in the jaws of the hammer so that sparks were struck from it as it met and tilted forward the steel frizzen. Falling into the now exposed pan, the sparks ignited the priming powder. There was a puff of white smoke from the pan and a tiny streak of flame passed through the touch-hole to detonate the main charge in the chamber. Spat out of the muzzle, the round lead ball flew to catch Sam in his right temple and burst out at the left. Pitched sideways, sam was dead before his body landed in the corner.

Having dealt with the Negro, the sergeant returned his gaze to Bowie and took note of his actions. Raising the rifle's butt above his shoulder, he drew it back so that he would be able to drive home the bayonet. Although the big *gringo's* right hand was closing on the hilt of the knife that protruded from the wall close to his head, the sergeant did not expect any difficulty in killing him. Handicapped as he was by the broken leg, the Texian seemed likely to be easy meat. Once he was dead, the sergeant would be able to claim the pistols and the knife as his loot.

Plucking his knife free as the burly, savage-featured Mexican bore down upon him, Bowie acted with the deadly speed which had made him famous and feared. Whipping the weapon around to the right before him, he directed its blade in an arc that was calculated to meet and deflect the attack.

Knife and bayonet converged before the latter, moving with all the sergeant's strength behind it, could reach its target. Such was the quality of the steel used by James Black to manufacture Bowie's already legendary weapon that its blade not only pushed aside, but actually cut into and snapped the greatly inferior metal of the bayonet when they came together.

Awe, amazement and alarm began to flood through the sergeant as he realized that in addition to his rifle being turned away from its intended mark, the bayonet had been snapped like a rotten twig. Before he could decide upon what defensive action he might take, his momentum carried him onwards to his death.

Having diverted the attack, Bowie rotated his right hand until its knuckles were pointing towards the floor. Even as the ruined bayonet went by him and impacted against the wall to halt its user, he chopped upwards in a circular motion to his left. Showing no evidence of having been dulled, or even affected, by its cutting into the bayonet, the blade sliced the lobe from the sergeant's left ear and gashed open the side of his neck. While painful, the injury was not fatal.

Realizing that he had not incapacitated his attacker, Bowie reversed the knife's direction. Passing beneath the sergeant's chin, the five-and-a-quarter-inch-long concave upper portion of the clip point made the contact. Being just as sharp as the main cutting edge, it laid his throat open to the bone. Blood spurted in a flood over Bowie's hand as he twisted the sergeant aside. Releasing the rifle, the dying man took a long, involuntary stride before he crumpled and went down.

At that moment, Lieutenant Arsenio Serrano arrived on the scene.

The son of a wealthy Northern Coahuila *haciendero*, Serrano was in his mid-twenties, tall, slender and good looking. Bare-headed, having lost his hat during the advance on the walls, his brown, waist-length, double-breasted shirt-jacket was decorated with silver braid and buttons. His brown, bell-bottomed trousers and spur-bearing boots seemed better suited to riding than marching.

With the ever-present threats posed by the local Yaqui Indians and frequent raiding by Comanches or Apaches from north of the *Rio Bravo*,[4] Don Pascual Serrano had insisted on retaining all his *vaqueros* to defend the *hacienda*. So his son had had to be content with taking twenty *peons* when he had gone to answer *Presidente* Santa Anna's call for support to quell the rebellion in Texas. That had meant he was given a commission in the Militia, instead of being allowed to join one of the elite volunteer cavalry regiments. Like all the Militia's officers, although he was fighting on foot, he had done all his travelling on horse-back while his men walked.

4. *Rio Bravo:* Mexicans' name for the Rio Grande.

If Arsenio Serrano had given thought to the matter, he might have considered himself a very lucky young man. Having been among the first arrivals outside the Alamo Mission, the Northern Coahuila Militia Regiment had suffered heavy casualties in the previous assaults. In fact, their strength had been so decimated by death, wounds and desertion that they could muster only two companies for the final attack. There had been a high mortality rate among the regiment's officers. The Texians and Crockett's Kentuckians were experienced Indian fighters and had known the strategic value of removing their enemies' leaders. Although Serrano had taken part in all the previous assaults and had had a few narrow escapes, he had come through them unscathed. That morning, because of their losses, his regiment had been held in reserve. So, much to his annoyance, Serrano had not reached the walls until after they had been breached.

On entering the plaza, hot and eager to play his part, Serrano had found that all the visible defenders were already being engaged in combat by the attackers who had preceded him. So he had led his men towards the hospital building. His luck had still held, although he did not regard it in that light. Flying from one of the savage, violent melees that were taking place all around the plaza, a bullet had struck his sword to shatter its blade and knock it from his hand. Surprise, alarm and not a little pain had caused him to drop his pistol and clutch at the stinging fingers with his left hand. While he had been delayed by retrieving and checking that the pistol had not lost the powder from its priming pan when it had struck the ground, Sergeant Ortega had led their men towards the hospital.

If it had not been for the chance destruction of the sword, Serrano and not the sergeant would have followed the two men into the room.

As it was, Serrano had seen the entry effected as he was running to join his men. He had watched Ortega following the pair who had broken open the door, heard the shots from inside and had witnessed the number of the party who had accompanied him from his home being reduced to four by the blast of Sam's shotgun. Calling upon the quartet to follow him, Serrano had set off to find out what was happening inside the building.

Having crowded through the door on their young officer's heels, the four *peons* were—like him—brought to a halt as they stared at the spectacle which was confronting them. There was something terrible and frightening about the big *gringo* who had, despite being incapacitated by his injury, already killed three of their number. If the grim, savage determination on his face was anything to go by, he was all too willing to continue with the slaughter.

Being descended from a family which had always produced brave fighting men, Serrano recovered quickly from the shock of his first real contact with one of the enemy. Up to that moment, they had always been at least a hundred yards away and no more than small, briefly seen shapes beyond the walls. So, momentarily, he had found coming into such sudden and close proximity to be disconcerting and alarming.

Then, having met Bowie at the home of a mutual friend, the young Mexican realized with whom they were dealing. For all his broken leg and even when armed only with that huge knife, Bowie would be a terribly dangerous adversary at close quarters.

With that in mind, Serrano raised and took aim along the barrel of his pistol. However, he could not bring himself to shoot without first having made what he guessed would be a futile and unacceptable demand for Bowie to surrender. As one of the men responsible for the rebellion, he would not allow himself to be taken alive.

Given what they regarded as guidance by the officer, the *peons* also lined their weapons at the big white man. If he was afraid of the rifles and pistol which were being pointed in his direction, he gave no sign of it. In fact, lifting the bloody knife in a menacing fashion, he swung his crutch forward as if he was meaning to advance and attack them.

"Surren—!" Serrano began, watching what Bowie was doing with something that was close to superstitious awe.

The feeling was duplicated by the *peons*. Before their officer could even complete the first word, the man at the left tightened his right forefinger and his weapon roared. His almost involuntary action proved to be infectious. With their nerves already stretched taut, the other Mexicans responded automatically. Three more rifles and the pistol thundered like a rolling echo to the first shot and clouds of smoke gushed from their muzzles. Eruptions of pulverized adobe on either side of Bowie showed that at least two of the men had missed. However, the rest were more fortunate.

Slammed away from the walls by the impact of the bullets— not one of which was smaller than .69 in caliber—ploughing into his head and torso, Bowie crashed to the floor. The knife left his hand and his fingers relaxed and slid almost to Serrano's feet. Wild with excitement that was mingled with relief and fear, the *peons* rushed forward. Time and again, their bayonets were thrust into the big Texan's body; but he could feel no pain.

Bending, Serrano picked up the knife. Although its handle was too large to be gripped comfortably with his fingers, he realized that he was holding a superlative example of the cutler's art. From outside, the noise of fighting was being replaced by cheers and shouts announcing that the enemy were finished. For a moment, Serrano felt disappointed over having been able to play only a minor part in the final battle of the siege. Then, looking at the knife which he was holding, he decided that he had still obtained a most worthwhile piece of loot.

What the young officer failed to appreciate was that something unique and *very* valuable had come into his possession. However, realizing that the knife would attract the envy of his superiors, he decided to keep it hidden and to avoid mentioning the part he had played in Bowie's death. By doing so, he hoped that he would be able to take it home with him at the end of the campaign.

CHAPTER TWO

It *Sounds* Straightforward Enough

"*Our family is willing to pay any reasonable price for the return of Uncle James's knife, which we now have good reason to believe is in Don Arsenio Serrano's possession. And so, sir, in view of the fact that you were able to render such a service to Don Arsenio, we feel that you may be able to help us in this matter. I cannot emphasize too strongly that we are not asking you to intercede directly on our behalf, but merely want your assistance in opening negotiations with Don Arsenio.*

"*I appreciate that your regretted disability will not allow you to visit Don Arsenio Serrano personally, but hope that you can see your way clear to allow a member of your family to accompany our representative, Mr. Octavius Xavier Guillemot. He will arrive at the Sandford Hotel in San Antonio de Bexar on, or about, April 24th and will await your answer.*

"*Mr. Guillemot has our full confidence and is empowered to carry out all necessary negotiations with Don Arsenio on our behalf. However, we and he believe that our request will*

*have more likelihood of receiving favorable attention if he can
be vouched for by you. That is why we would like the services
of your personal, accredited representative.*

*"In view of the unusual nature of this request, I offer as
proof of my bona fides the fact that my father told me, in the
strictest confidence, of the part Miss Melissa Cornforth played
in the incident at Crown Bayou.*

*"Trusting that you will give this matter your consideration
and that we may look forward to a favorable reply,*

Sir, I remain,

Yours in anticipation,

Resin Bowie II."

Having read aloud for a second time the most relevant portion of the letter which had just been delivered from the post
office at Polveroso City, seat of Rio Hondo County, General
Jackson Baines Hardin—who was better known as "Ole
Devil"—raised his eyes and looked, without really seeing, at
the other occupant of the comfortably furnished, gun-decorated
study in the OD Connected ranch's main house.

In his mind's eye, Ole Devil was picturing a valley about
five miles north of Eagle Pass about thirty-nine years earlier.
A group of Texian hard-cases had been on the point of mur-
dering a young Mexican Militia officer whom they had captured
as he was fleeing from the Battle of San Jacinto[1] and trying to
return to his home below the border. Ole Devil and a small
party of the Texas Light Cavalry, who had been attending to
a confidential assignment for Major General Samuel Houston,
had arrived and intervened.[2] Ole Devil had been compelled to
kill the leader of the mob before they would disperse. Introducing himself, Lieutenant Arsenio Serrano had thanked Ole
Devil for saving his life. As the two young men had shaken
hands, each had known that a debt had been incurred. If at any
time in the future Ole Devil chose to ask for something in
return, he had felt sure that Serrano would give it without
hesitation. On giving his parole not to take up arms against the
Texians in the future, Serrano had been loaned a horse and

1. April 20th, 1836.
2. What the assignment was is told in: *Get Urrea.*

pistol to replace those which he had lost and allowed to go on
his way.

The years since the meeting had been very full for Ole Devil
Hardin. They had been action-packed and eventful years, in
which he had fulfilled the promise which he had already been
showing of becoming a prominent factor in the affairs of Texas.
Nor had being crippled in a riding accident and confined to a
wheel-chair[3] shortly after the War Between The States—in
which he had played a not inconsiderable part as a general in
the Confederate States' Army—lessened to any great extent
the influence which he had come to wield.

It is probable that Serrano would have recognized his rescuer
if they had met. In spite of the accident, Ole Devil had aged
gracefully and with little change. While the once black hair
was now grey, the lean face's crooked eyebrows and aquiline
nose still gave it a Mephistophelian aspect which in part had
been responsible for his nickname.[4] The strong features displayed no bitterness or despair over the disability but for which
he might have held high public office in the State of Texas.
His lean body might be wrapped in a blanket from the waist
down, but the shoulders under his dark-blue smoking jacket
retained much of their military stiffness.

"Well, Dustine?" Ole Devil said, laying the letter on the
table. "What do you make of it?"

The young man to whom the question had been addressed
had attained much the same position in comparison with Ole
Devil, in the esteem of their fellow Texans—the "i" having
been deleted from the name after independence had been won
from Mexico—as Ole Devil had been to James Bowie, William
Barrett Travis, General Houston or Davy Crockett back in the
mid-1830s. Yet, taking into consideration the reputation which
Captain Dustine Edward Marsden Fog had earned during the
War Between The States and since,[5] his physical appearance
was mighty deceptive. By popular conception, a man capable
of the deeds which he had performed should have been a ver-
itable giant and exceptionally handsome to boot.

3. Told in the "The Paint" episode of: *The Fastest Gun in Texas*.
4. Another reason was the reputation he had gained for being a "lil ole devil
in a fight."
5. Details of Dusty Fog's history and special qualifications are given in
Appendix 1.

Not quite five foot six inches in height, Dusty Fog had a tanned, reasonably good-looking face which was far from impressive when in repose and curly, dusty blond hair. Although his clothing—that of a working cowhand—tended to hide rather than show it off, he had the muscular development of a Hercules in miniature. His garments were functional, of excellent cut and quality, but he contrived to make them look like somebody else's cast-offs. Even when wearing his gunbelt—which he was not at that moment—with the matched, bone-handled Colt Civilian Model Peacemakers in the cross-draw holsters, he was likely to go unnoticed unless danger threatened. *Then* his true potential suddenly became all too obvious.

Not that Ole Devil needed any convincing about the capability of the young man who was his *segundo*, the leader of his ranch's floating outfit[6] and his favorite—although he would never admit it in so many words—nephew.

"It *sounds* straightforward enough, sir," Dusty replied, his voice a quiet, well-educated Texas drawl. "Only I seem to remember when Tommy used to tell us about you rescuing *Senior* Serrano, he always allowed that he wasn't armed and you had to lend him a pistol."

"I did," Ole Devil agreed, knowing that his Japanese valet—who had been on the mission—had told the story to the younger members of the Hardin, Fog and Blaze clan.

"Then it doesn't seem likely that he could have had Colonel Bowie's knife with him," Dusty stated. "Lon's old toad-sticker was made by James Black to Colonel Bowie's pattern. If it is anything to go by, *Senor* Serrano couldn't've been wearing it, even hidden under his clothes, without you seeing it."

"It could have been in his saddlebags," Ole Devil pointed out. "A young officer wouldn't want to show off such a valuable piece of loot for fear that one of his superiors, or even Santa Anna, would take it from him. He explained that he wasn't armed as he hadn't thought it would be necessary, he was only going to ride across and take breakfast with a friend who'd arrived the night before with Cos's column. His horse bolted when the powder wagon we'd set a fuse in blew up and, by the time he'd brought it back under control, the battle was so

6. New readers can find an explanation of a floating outfit's function and purpose in Appendix 2.

close to over that he knew it would be no use going back. So he set off for home."

"Hadn't the fellers who'd caught him searched the saddle-bags?"

"No. We arrived before they could. And, as we weren't after loot, we didn't bother. He explained why he wasn't armed. They'd shot his horse from under him, so I lent him another and turned him loose."

"Then he could have had it, sir," Dusty admitted, showing no surprise at his uncle's chivalrous behavior. It was what he expected of Ole Devil Hardin. "Thing that puzzles me, though, is why the Bowie family have waited for so long before trying to get the knife back?"

"According to the letter, they've only just recently learned of its whereabouts."

"Didn't they try to find out what had happened to it when they first heard of Colonel's Bowie's death?"

"They could have and probably did," Ole Devil admitted, "although I never got to hear about it."

"Didn't *you* ever wonder what had happened to it, sir?" Dusty inquired.

"I suppose that it must have crossed my mind at some time or another," Ole Devil answered. "But I had plenty other, more important things on it in the days that followed the Alamo. Probably I was like everybody else and accepted that it had been carried off by whoever had killed him. I wasn't at San Jacinto for long after the battle. Then before I'd rejoined General Houston after settling accounts with Urrea, Santa Anna and his army had left Texas and there were other things needing my attention. If it comes to a point, I never even heard who had killed Bowie. Houston wouldn't allow any extensive investigation into that aspect of the siege, so that he could avoid refusing demands for reprisals against the men concerned. I suppose that Serrano could have been responsible, he admitted to having been at the Alamo."

"Peña, Navarro and the others whose accounts of the siege I've read never named him as Colonel Bowie's killer,"[7] Dusty

7. Colonel José Enrique de la Peña, Captain Sánchez Navarro, Colonel Almonte, Captain Fernando Urizza and other Mexican officers published statements, or stories, about the siege, and these were translated and circulated in Texas.

said pensively. "But, especially after word got around about how you dealt with Urrea, they could have had much the same notion in mind as General Houston about avoiding reprisals and kept quiet."

"That's true. Or, if I was right about why he was hiding the knife, they wouldn't have known," Ole Devil replied.

"You never saw him again, sir?"

"No. He sent back the horse and pistol, along with a message saying that I'd always be welcome if I cared to visit *Casa* Serrano and explaining how to get there. I had a letter during the Mexican War assuring me that he'd honored his word and hadn't taken up arms against Texas. We've written back and forth maybe a dozen times since then, but I never got around to paying him a visit."

"Huh huh," Dusty grunted, then another thought struck him. "I wonder how the Bowies learned about you helping *Senor* Serrano?"

"Well, I've never made any special effort to keep it a secret, although there was never an official written report about the mission I was on when we met," Ole Devil answered. "There were eight of us on it. One of the others might have mentioned what happened, but I've never hear of it if they did."

"I've never come across any mention of it in a book, sir," Dusty declared. "Not that I could lay claim to having read everything which's been written about that period. Thing being, what're you going to do about this letter, sir?"

"Like it reminds me in the paragraph about the incident at Crown Bayou being verification of his *bona fides,* I owe the Bowie family a favor," Ole Devil replied. "And what they're asking of me doesn't seem too much in repayment. All they want is for me to help get their man to *Casa* Serrano and vouch for them having sent him."

"Which'll be easy enough done," Dusty said quietly. "Just so long as the Bowie family *did* send him."

"How do you mean?" Ole Devil wanted to know, although he guessed that his nephew was duplicating his own line of reasoning.

"How can we be sure that this letter's really from Resin Bowie the Second, sir?" Dusty challenged, tapping the sheet of paper with his right forefinger and unconsciously confirming his uncle's judgement.

"Why wouldn't it be?"

"Jim Bowie's original knife would be a mighty interesting curio, sir, and *real* valuable. It'd be something any collector would pay mighty high to lay his hands on. Or go to some trouble to get hold of."

"That's true enough," Ole Devil conceded. "I've never met Resin Bowie the Second, or had cause to get to know his handwriting. I can't even be sure that this is his real address, although it was posted in Baton Rouge, his father's home town. On the other hand, he knows about what happened at Crown Bayou. Some of it's been made public, but not about Melissa Cornforth's part in it. Only myself and the Bowie brothers knew that she was involved. So I'm inclined to believe that the letter is genuine. In which case, I'm honor bound to do as he asks."

"He could've picked a better time to ask for help, sir," Dusty drawled, accepting the decision without question and starting to consider how to have it carried out. "Cousin Red and Mark[8] aren't back from delivering that herd to fill our Army beef contract. Waco's pulled out yesterday to help Tom Blevins up to Clinton City.[9] Not that it's going to need all of them. Lon's not doing anything, except rile Cousin Betty.[10] so I could send him."

"You're my nephew and my segundo, Dustine," Ole Devil pointed out. "The letter asks me to send a member of my family. Even if it didn't, it would be more tactful and polite if I have you there to speak for me."

"It would, sir," Dusty agreed. "There's nothing happening around the spread that needs me to handle it. I can leave tomorrow and be in San Antonio by the twenty-fourth, even without pushing my horse—Damn it!"

"What's wrong?" Ole Devil asked, as his nephew uttered

8. Red Blaze and Mark Counter, members of the OD Connected's ranch crew who appear in various books from the "Floating Outfit" series.

9. Waco, youngest member of Ole Devil's floating outfit. What his task in Clinton City entailed is told in the "The Hired Butcher" episode of *The Hard Riders* and the "A Tolerable Straight Shooting Gun" episode of *The Floating Outfit*. He later became a well-known peace officer, as is told in the "Waco" series of books.

10. Betty Hardin; Ole Devil's granddaughter. She takes a prominent part in: *Kill Dusty Fog, The Bad Bunch, McGraw's Inheritance, The Rio Hondo War* and *Gunsmoke Thunder*.

the last two words with an expression of annoyance.

"I'd clean forgotten for the moment, sir. But Colin Far-quharson's[11] bringing in some of his best mares to be bred, and he'll be here before I can get back."

"You don't need to be here for that. Betty and Colin can handle it."

She'd probably say better than with me here," Dusty grinned, for his cousin was a high-spirited and very capable young lady. "But I won't be able to use my paint. He's one of the stallions that Colin's wanting to use for stud."

"Can't you take one of the other horses from your mount?"[12] Ole Devil inquired.

"Yes, sir," Dusty conceded. "There's that big claybank gelding I've just taken in. He's not trained for cattle work, but he's got stamina to burn and a bit of hard work won't do him any harm."

"I'll leave that to you," Ole Devil stated. "Now, while I'm nearly certain that this letter is genuine, it might not be. So I'll send a telegraph to Resin Bowie the Second—"

"It'll be at least two days before we can hope for an answer, sir," Dusty reminded his uncle respectfully, although he was sure that the point had already been considered. "Even riding relay, I couldn't reach San Antonio by the twenty-fourth if I wait until it comes."

"There's no need for you to wait here for the answer," Ole Devil replied. "The Bowies seem to think highly of this Octavius Xavier Guillemot—"

"Like Lon'll probably say," Dusty drawled. "There's a mighty high-toned name."

"Very impressive," Ole Devil admitted with a frosty grin. "Don't let it influence you when you're sizing him up, which I want you to do *very* carefully. If you're satisfied, take him to *Casa* Serrano and fetch him back safely to San Antonio, with or without the knife."

"Yo!" Dusty answered, employing the cavalry's traditional response to an order.

"I'll forward the answer to my message and it will be waiting

11. Colin Farquharson's connection with the floating outfit is told in: .44 *Caliber Man* and *A Horse Called Mogollon*.
12. Most Texans used the word "mount" for their string of work horses.

waiting for you at the Sandford Hotel on your return," Ole
Devil went on. "You can take whatever action you consider
necessary after you've read it."

"Yes, sir," Dusty said thoughtfully, and his gaze went to
where his gunbelt was laying on a small table near the door.
"Only, if the letter is a fake, this Guillemot feller's not going
to be too eager to hand over the knife."

"That's true," Ole Devil conceded, following the direction
in which the small Texan was looking and guessing what he
had in mind. "However, the letter doesn't say I shouldn't send
more than one man. And, after all, even if it is genuine, Guillemot's likely to be fresh from east of the Mississippi River
and new to the West. You've got some mighty rough country
to cross between San Antonio and *Casa* Serrano. The Ysabel
Kid knows Mexico and would be very useful as a guide."

"I was thinking that myself, sir," Dusty admitted, then
grinned. "Only Lon's not going to be any too pleased when
he hears about it?"

"Why not?" Ole Devil challenged. "He's always complain-
ing about having to be around the ranch."

"Yes, sir," Dusty replied. "But Colin's using his old Blackie
horse as a stud, too."

CHAPTER THREE

Somebody's Laying For Us

"Wouldn't want to go a-worrying you, Dusty, it being such a pleasant afternoon 'n' all," the Ysabel Kid remarked, showing no change in his conversational tone nor difference in the re-laxed posture with which he was sitting the big brown, spot-rumped Appaloosa gelding that he was riding instead of his magnificent white stallion. "But I just saw somebody peeking at us from the top of that right-hand knob ahead."

Without making his actions obvious, Dusty Fog looked in the required direction. The terrain over which he and his com-panion were passing, following the stagecoach trail that ran roughly north-west from Polveroso City to San Antonio de Bexar—a distance of slightly over one hundred miles—was typical open range for that part of Texas. Mainly grassland, it was scarred by coulees and draws as well as being punctuated by numerous rocky outcrops, clumps of bushes and groves of trees. Although the small Texan studied the "knob" to which his companion had referred, he failed to detect the watcher.

"He's not there now," Dusty declared, sitting his sixteen-hand claybank[1] gelding with an equally relaxed and effortless-seeming grace.

"Nope," the Kid agreed. "Just come up and ducked down again *pronto*."

"Land's sakes," Dusty ejaculated. "I never did see such an all-fired suspicious-natured and untrusting a feller as you, Lon. We're not yet thirty miles from home and you're already figuring that somebody's laying for us."

"I was born and raised that way," the Kid answered. "And staying like it's helped me to keep on living so's I'll grow to be old, honored and respected."

"Honored and *respected!*" Dusty repeated, almost snorting the words out. "That damned old *you* could *never* live to be."

Despite the undertone of friendly derision in the small Texan's voice, he did not dismiss his companion's warning as being unworthy of serious consideration. Nor, despite the "knob" being over half a mile away, did he doubt that the Kid had seen somebody looking at them over the top of it. As well as having instilled a sense of alert, wary and ever-watchful caution into him, the Kid's upbringing and early training had left him with an exceptionally keen eye-sight and powers of observation of a high quality.[2]

While Dusty did not have any reason to anticipate trouble, particularly so close to home—they had only gone about a mile beyond the stream which formed the boundary of Rio Hondo County—he knew that he and the other members of the floating outfit had made a number of enemies; any of whom would be willing to try to take revenge if presented with an opportunity. However, if an attempt was to be made upon their lives, he could not ask for better, more loyal, nor capable backing.

Black haired, around six foot in height, lean as a steer that had grown up in the greasewood country and possessing much the same kind of wiry, tireless strength and endurance, Loncey Dalton Ysabel—to give the Kid his full name—was a fighting *man* second to none. Yet, as in Dusty's case, first appearances

1. Claybank: a yellowish color produced from breeding a sorrel and a dun.
2. Details of the Ysabel Kid's history and special qualifications are given in Appendix 2.

could be very misleading. The Kid's Indian-dark, handsome face, with its expression of almost babyish innocence, seemed young and harmless. A closer examination of his red-hazel eyes, or his features in times of stress, gave a warning that the innocence, like beauty, was only skin deep.

From the low-crowned, wide-brimmed J. B. Stetson hat tilted at a jack-deuce angle on his head, through bandana, shirt, vest and trousers to his low-heeled boots, the Kid's attire was black in color as if to match his hair. Even his gunbelt, with an old Colt Model of 1848 Dragoon revolver butt forward in a low cavalry-twist holster at the right and an ivory-handled James Black bowie knife sheathed on the left, was of the same hue. A Winchester Model of 1866 rifle was cradled across his bent left arm. The lead-rope of a pack-horse, carrying Dusty's and his bed rolls and supplies, was secured to the low horn of his double-girthed[3] range saddle.

"Maybe not; company's I'm keeping these days," the Kid conceded, favoring the small Texan with a quick and pointed glance before continuing his scrutiny of the "knob." But I sure's hell don't aim to change my ways none."

"That's what I meant," Dusty countered, raising his left hand to thumb back his black Stetson. "He alone, or does he have some *amigos* on hand?"

"If he has, I don't see 'em," the Kid answered, transferring his attention from the "knob" to a similar rocky outcrop at about the same distance—slightly over two hundred yards— from the left-hand side of the trail. "But I'm willing to bet there'll be at least one more up there. I could cut around a ways and scout a mite."

"It wouldn't do any good," Dusty objected. "If it is somebody wanting to do a meanness to us, they'd see what you're fixing to do and light out. I'd sooner have them stay put and get it over with than have the worry of who they might be and when they'll be making another stab at killing us."

"And me," the Kid admitted.

While speaking, the Kid was hooking the Appaloosa's loose-hanging reins over the first and second fingers of his left hand. Still keeping his movements just as unobtrusive, he unfastened

3. Because of its Mexican connotations, few Texans used the word 'cinch'.

the lead rope's knot and replaced it with a dally.[4] By doing so, he knew that he could part company with the pack-horse in a hurry if necessary. However, he did not follow a dally-roper's practice of retaining the loose end in his hand. The horse was sufficiently well trained to accompany the Appaloosa and would neither hang back nor attempt to pull free under normal conditions.

With the dally applied, the Kid let his right hand move in a casual-seeming manner until it enfolded the wrist of the Winchester's butt and its finger entered the triggerguard and the ring of the loading lever.

"It's lucky you've already got your rifle out," Dusty remarked, having watched the precautions with approval.

Apart from the twin outcrops, there was little cover closer than a quarter of a mile on each side of the trail. Certainly none in which an enemy, knowing with whom he was dealing, would care to entrust himself when laying even an impromptu and unanticipated ambush which would involve the Ysabel Kid. So the would-be assailants were almost sure to be at a distance over which a revolver, even in Dusty's expert hands, would be hard put to make a hit. For the Kid to have drawn his rifle from its saddleboot without having any apparent reason to do so would have warned the watcher that his presence had been detected.

"Lucky!" the Kid yelped, adopting the air of one whose virtue had been maligned. "I did it so's I could do a kindness for a friend 'n' feller Texan."

For all the banter, the Kid secretly agreed with Dusty that it was fortunate he had the rifle in such a readily accessible position. Normally, unless he had reason for expecting to need it, it would have been in the saddleboot under his left leg with the butt pointing to the rear for easy withdrawal on dismounting. However, they had heard that Watson Weller—an old friend and owner of the stagecoach relay station at which they were planning to spend the night—was being plagued by a pack of Texas grey wolves. Having found signs that the animals had

---

4. Dally: to take a half-hitch around the saddlehorn, usually after a catch has been made, so that the rope can be released quickly in an emergency. Texans rarely employed a dally when roping, preferring to "tie-fast" with a knot and so hang on to their captive no matter what happened.

been on the bank of the boundary stream recently, he had drawn his Winchester ready for use if he should see them.

Although the opportunity to help rid Weller of the troublesome animals had not presented itself, the Kid's willingness to help was paying an unexpected dividend. If he and Dusty should be attacked, he was already holding the means with which he could start fighting back immediately. That would allow the small Texan to extract the new Winchester Model of 1873 from his saddleboot and bring it into use.

As the Kid had claimed, his education as one of the *Pehnane*—Quick-Stinger, Wasp, or Raider—Commanche band had taught him the value of constant vigilance. Nor had the events in his subsequent life been calculated to have reduced his faith in the lessons of his childhood, rather they had tended to sharpen his appreciation of what he had learned. So, holding the Appaloosa and packhorse to a pace which matched that of his companion's claybank, he continued to scour the terrain ahead with eyes which had won him acclaim in the Comanches' training game of *Nanip'ka*.[5]

How'd you handle it, was you laying for somebody from them?" Dusty inquired, studying the outcrops with the eye of a strategist.

"That'd depend on how many he was, what kind of rifles we'd got and *who* we was laying for," the Kid replied. "Less we'd got buffalo guns and could count on making a hit—knowing who we're after—I'd let you and me get by and take us from behind."

"That's how I see it," Dusty admitted. "Knowing it's *you* they're tangling with, they'd not want to chance showing themselves as we're riding towards them."

"So how do we play it, *amigo?*" the Kid wanted to know, accepting the compliment with becoming false modesty.

"There's only one way, happen they don't show their hand sooner," Dusty decided soberly. "Keep riding until we're right between them, then use our spurs and go like the devil after a yearling."

"Sounds reasonable," the Kid drawled. "Only let's sort of spread out a mite."

5. A description of how to play *Nanip'ka*, "Guess Over The Hill," is given in *Comanche*.

Accepting his companion's suggestion, Dusty set about implementing it. As they continued to ride along at the same leisurely pace, giving little visible evidence of their watchfulness, they gradually separated until they had the width of the trail between them. Apart from that, to the watchers, it would have appeared that they were completely unaware of their danger.

However, Dusty and the Kid kept their eyes constantly on the move. Being skilled fighting men, at no time were they both looking in the same direction. While the Kid was subjecting the terrain on the left to his eagle-eyed and Comanche-trained scrutiny, Dusty was watching the right. When the Indian-dark youngster turned his gaze in that direction, the small Texan kept the left-hand outcrop under observation.

"I'm damned if I can see 'em," the Kid stated in an aggrieved fashion, as he and Dusty were within fifty yards of passing between the outcrops. "And I'll *never* hear the end of it happen I was wrong about seeing—"

As if wishing to save the young Texan from such an embarrassment, a man rose from where he had been crouching in concealment on top of the left-hand outcrop. In doing so, he was ignoring the instructions which he had been given by his companion across the trail. While he had refrained from stating his objections, he had not approved of the way in which they were supposed to act. So, instead of allowing their victims to pass by before opening fire, he stood up. He was raising his rifle towards his shoulder when he realized that he had underestimated the caliber of the men he was up against.

The moment that he saw the top of the man's high-crowned *sombrero* appearing, the Kid started to swing up his Winchester. While doing so, he shook free the reins and, as they fell, his right toe tapped the Appaloosa's right shoulder in the signal which he had taught it to mean "halt." Although the gelding obeyed instantly, the pack-horse continued to walk by on the left.

Catching a movement on the summit of the right side's outcrop and noticing the Kid's behavior, Dusty set into motion the plan of action which he had decided upon. Slipping his right foot from the stirrup iron, he swung it to the rear. He intended to drop to the ground and slide the carbine from its boot.

Moving with smoothly-flowing speed, the Kid lined his sights and, when satisfied—which only took just over a second—he tightened his right forefinger. There was a crack as the waiting bullet was detonated. Down and up swung the loading lever, to toss out the empty cartridge case, cock the hammer and replenish the chamber in a single motion. Again and for a third time, making a small alteration to its point of aim between them, the Winchester flung out a .44 caliber bullet. Through the powder-smoke, he saw the slender, *charro*-dressed figure on the outcrop jerk violently. Firing his rifle into the air, the man twirled around and tumbled from view. The Kid could not have said which of his bullets had found its mark. Nor did he give the matter much thought.

The danger was not yet over, and Dusty was in serious trouble!

While the small Texan's plans for dealing with the situation were basically sound, he had made one miscalculation. He had failed to take into consideration that he was *not* riding his reliable and trustworthy paint stallion.

Unused to having firearms discharged so close to it, the claybank gelding gave an alarmed snort and made a violent rearing plunge forward as the Kid's Winchester went off. Caught unawares, with his right leg passing over the cantle of the saddle and his torso inclined to the left ready to dismount, Dusty felt the horn snatched from beneath his left hand. Deprived of that support, there was no way, excellent rider though he was, in which he could prevent himself from being thrown. In fact, he had barely time to snatch his left foot out of its stirrup and release the reins before he was pitched sideways. Trying to break his fall, as the horse bolted, he crashed to the ground. A searing agony numbed his senses as his ribs struck a boulder and all the breath was driven from his body, leaving him numb and helpless.

Although the Kid was aware of what had happened, he could not attempt to ascertain the extent of his *amigo's* injuries. Not while he was conscious of the possibility of there being other assailants to be accounted for.

Realizing that Dusty would not be able to do so, the Kid set about dealing with the problem. Part of the Appaloosa's training had been to accept being mounted or dismounted on the right as well as from the left. Taking advantage of that fact, the Kid slipped his left foot from the stirrup and swung it forward and up without taking the butt of the Winchester from his shoulder or his left hand off the wooden foregrip. As he did so, the wisdom of his having changed the means of securing the pack-horse proved its worth.

Like Dusty's claybank, the pack-horse was displaying its resentment over the shooting. However it was backing away instead of running forward and, but for the precautions taken by the Kid, would have prevented him from carrying out his scheme. Rising so as to pass over the saddlehorn, his left leg hit the lead-rope. A knot would have held, but the half-hitch of the dally performed its function by giving way. Freeing his other foot as the leg thrust the rope aside, the Kid leapt to the ground. He not only alighted facing in the required direction, but with his rifle still held ready for use.

Slanting the Winchester upwards, the Kid saw that there was a figure sky-lined at the top of the right side outcrop. Clad in Mexican fashion like his companion, he was still in the process of raising his rifle.

Something about the man struck the Kid as being vaguely familiar. However, he was not given the opportunity to make an accurate identification. Clearly the man had a healthy respect for his ability with a Winchester. Without making any attempt to use his own weapon, he swung around and, before the Kid could draw a bead on him, sprang back out of sight.

The man's abrupt departure placed the Kid on the horns of a dilemma. While his first inclination was to go and make sure that their assailant did not mean to resume the attack from another position, he also wanted to find out if his *amigo* had been seriously injured. The latter impulse won, but he did not permit his anxiety to override caution. Lowering his rifle, but holding it ready to be raised and used if the need arose, he backed across the trail. He continued to keep the outcrop under observation until he was by Dusty's side. Looking down, he found to his relief that the small Texan was conscious.

"How bad is it?" the Kid asked and the concern in his voice was not simulated.

"I—I—think—bust—some—ribs!" Dusty gasped, rolling on to his back with his right hand pressed against his left side. Although his face showed he was in agony, he tried to sit up and looked at the outcrop. "Wh—where's—the—feller?"

"He lit out," the Kid replied.

"Best—take—after—him," Dusty gritted. "I—'ll—make—out—until—you've—made—sure—he's—not—about—to—come—back."

"I'll tend to it," the Kid promised, glancing to where the claybank was still running. However, the pack-horse had not gone far and was grazing at the side of the trail. "Don't you go 'way, mind."

Much as the Kid wished he could give his *amigo*'s injuries immediate attention, he was equally aware that their remaining attacker might be lurking in the vicinity to try to finish off his work. Collecting the Appaloosa, he fastened its reins to the saddlehorn and guided it with his legs so as to leave his hands free for handling the Winchester.

Although the Kid was ready to take any action which might become necessary, none was called for. On passing around the side of the outcrop, he found that the man apparently did not intend to renew hostilities in the immediate future. Nor had he wasted any time since diving out of sight. He was already galloping away as fast as his horse would carry him and did not even look back.

Realizing that the man had already built up such a lead that any attempt to catch him would entail a long chase, the Kid signalled for his Appaloosa to halt. Although the horse stood like a rock as he snapped the butt of the Winchester to his shoulder, he did not fire. He knew that, with the would-be attacker at least half a mile away and travelling at such a place, he could only expect to make a hit if he took very careful aim. Before he could do so, the man had disappeared into a coulee. By the time he had emerged, he was far out of range and still riding at a gallop.

"Go on, you bastard, keep running!" the Kid growled disgustedly and lowered the Winchester. "There's not a thing I can do about you right now. I just hope that you come back for seconds, so's I can find out if I *do* know you."

Having made the comment, the Kid looked for Dusty's horse. Although it had slowed down, the claybank was still running. Letting out a curse over the animal's behavior, he reached for the Appaloosa's reins with the intention of untying them. Even as he did so, he saw a man riding from a clump of trees on the other side of the trail and heading to cut off the claybank. On the point of raising the Winchester, the Kid refrained from doing so when he identified the newcomer.

However, despite recognizing Watson Weller, the Kid knew that he still could not pursue the departing attacker. Much as he would have liked to satisfy his curiosity, he accepted that it would not be possible under the circumstances. If Dusty was correct in his diagnosis, he would not be able to complete the assignment they were engaged upon. In all probability, the Kid would have to handle it for him. Otherwise, the Kid could have set off after the man, relying upon the Appaloosa's speed and endurance, or his own skill at following tracks, to bring them together. As it was, he reluctantly conceded that he would have to let the other get away.

"I just wish I knowed who you was and why you was after us," the Kid mused, riding to meet Weller—who had caught the claybank and was approaching. Then another thought struck him. "And how the hell did you know we'd be using this trail today?"

CHAPTER FOUR

Don't Kill Him Just Yet

"Why howdy there, Kid, I ain't seen you-all in a coon's age," greeted the bald-headed old hostler of Shelby's Livery Barn on the fringes of San Antonio de Bexar, beaming delightedly at the trail-dirty young man who was walking out of the darkness leading a big Appaloosa gelding. "How's General Hardin, Cap'n Fog 'n' all the folks back home to the OD Connected?"

"Fit's frog's hair, most of 'em, Milt," the Ysabel Kid replied, although he wished that the hostler had drawn the correct conclusion regarding the manner in which he was dressed and had refrained from announcing his identity so openly.

Watson Weller had been hunting for the pack of wolves when he had heard the shooting. On joining the Kid and learning what had caused it, he had forgotten all about the animals. While the Kid had gone to examine the man he had shot, Weller had attended to Dusty Fog. As the small Texan had suspected, three of his ribs were cracked. Fortunately, there had been no more serious internal damage.

When the Kid had arrived to say that his victim appeared
to be of mixed American–Mexican parentage, but was carrying
nothing to identify him or suggest why he had taken part in the
attack, Weller had been able to furnish some information. He
had said that the young man had arrived at his relay station
late the previous afternoon, accompanied by another half-breed;
a *pistolero valiente* called Matteo Urizza, who the Kid knew
slightly. They had taken a room for the night and left shortly
after breakfast that morning. Although Urizza had called his
companion "Enrique," Weller had not learned his surname. As
far as he was aware, they had asked no questions about other
users of the trail. While they had studied the horses in the
corrals and barn and had shown interest every time anybody
had entered the house, he had put that down to nothing more
than the watchful nature that was a vital necessity in their line
of work.

On hearing why the ambush had failed, Weller had declared
that he was not surprised by "Enrique's" behavior. He had
struck the old timer as being eager to prove that he was a real
bad *hombre*. Such a man might have considered that, although
he was going up against Dusty Fog and the Ysabel Kid—or
perhaps even because of *who* they were—he did not want to
follow the comparatively safe and easy course that had been
proposed by his more experienced and cautious companion.

While awaiting Weller's return with the buckboard which
he had gone to fetch from his relay station, to transport Dusty—
who was unable to ride—there, the two young Texans had
dismissed the ambush. On learning from the Kid that Urizza
made his headquarters in Rosa Rio's notorious *cantina* at San
Antonio, Dusty had wondered if the letter received by his uncle
was merely intended to lead them into a trap. Although the
contingency might have been remote, they had considered it
as explaining how Urizza could have known they would probably be on the trail. He would have reasoned that, if Ole Devil
had agreed to do as "Resin Bowie II" had requested, the men
who were to carry out the assignment would leave the OD
Connected shortly after the letter's arrival. As the stagecoach
which delivered the mail from San Antonio had reached Polveroso City the previous day, Urizza would expect his would-
be victims to be approaching Weller's relay station during the

afternoon and had laid his ambush accordingly. That he had merely been contemplating a robbery of the first travellers to pass was out of the question. While his and Enrique's horses had been hidden from the view of riders approaching from Rio Hondo County, they would have been seen by anybody who was coming from the other direction.

Another possible explanation for the attempt had occurred to Dusty and the Kid. The letter was genuine, but somebody did not want Ole Devil's representatives to contact Octavius Xavier Guillemot. If that was the case, it would clear up the point of why only two men had been involved in the abortive interception. Such an apparently simple task would hardly warrant the services of the whole floating outfit. In fact, particularly as spring was always an exceptionally busy period on a ranch, probably only one, or at the most two of them would be dispatched by Ole Devil.

With that possibility in mind, it had been decided that the Kid should take a few precautions during the remainder of the journey. Although Urizza had fled, he might obtain assistance and try again. Or there might be other men with similar orders watching the trail. To lessen the chances of being recognized at a distance, the Kid was to change his all-black garments for a grey shirt, multi-colored bandana and a pair of old Levi's trousers. He always carried the spare clothing in his war bag, so that it could be used for a similar purpose. He worked on the assumption that by the time he was close enough for his Stetson or armament to be identified he would already have located whoever was studying him.

Having spent the night at the relay station, the Kid had set off for San Antonio the following morning. He had left the pack-horse behind, preferring to travel light, carrying his bed roll strapped to the cantle of his saddle. Not only did he have a copy of Bowie's letter and the letter of introduction which Ole Devil had written to Don Arsenio Serrano, but Dusty had given him a note which would explain to Guillemot who he was and what had happened. His instructions were basically those which Dusty had received from Ole Devil and he had been confident that he could carry them out.

The journey to San Antonio had been so uneventful that the Kid might have—but did not—considered the change of attire a waste of time. Except when approaching a relay station, he had travelled parallel to the trail at a distance of around half a mile. His visits to the stations had been of short duration, merely long enough for him to take a meal and to acquire what in every case had proved to be almost negative information. While Urizza and his companion had passed through, even less was known about their purpose than Weller had discovered and the *pistolero valiente* had not called in on his return journey. If he had picked up another helper, so that he could make another attempt at earning his pay—he had had no personal reason for wanting to kill either Dusty or the Kid—there had been no mention of it. Nor had the Kid discovered anything to have led him to assume that other men were hoping to intercept him. The Kid's arrivals had aroused no curiosity. Like Weller, the men with whom he had talked had assumed that he was going to San Antonio to enjoy the festivities of the Bexar County Fair which was in progress.

Refusing to allow himself to be lulled into a sense of false security by the lack of hostile activity, the Kid had decided against resuming his all-black clothing for the time being. He had also considered it was advisable to delay his entrance into the city until after nightfall.

Not until the Kid had been approaching Shelby's Livery Barn had he wondered if he might be making a mistake by going there. The floating outfit always used it when in San Antonio. However, he had balanced the chance of anybody who was looking for him knowing that against other factors. With so many people in town for the County Fair, all such places would be filled. If it was at all possible, Shelby's staff would find accommodation for the Appaloosa. In addition, he would be among friends there and they would warn him of any danger. Lastly—and not the least important to his way of thinking—he could rely upon his horse being well cared for.

"Got any room for this fool critter, Milt?" the Kid inquired, glancing around.

Apart from one other person, the Kid and the hostler had the big building to themselves. A thin, unshaven and poorly dressed man was staring at the newcomer while sluggishly sweeping the floor with a broom. He looked like a typical range-town idler, the kind who could be found swamping a saloon or performing any such menial task which required neither skill nor a great deal of effort.

"You can have that 'n'," Milt answered, indicating an empty stall. "T'other empty 'n's took already. Hey though, where's your ole Blackie hoss?"

"Left him back to home, having his pleasure with a bunch of Colin Farquharson's mares," the Kid replied, making his way towards the designated stall.

"Is this'n 's mean 'n' ornery's that big white goat?" Milt inquired, eyeing the Appaloosa with wary caution as it approached on its master's heels.

"Nigh on, but not quite."

"That being the case, I'm staying well clear of him. Is anybody else coming down from the spread?"

"Nobody. What with the spring round up and all, they're all needed. I sort of snuck off. Looks like you're keeping busy."

"Town's busting at the seams," Milt admitted, closing the gate behind his visitor and the Appaloosa. "You got someplace in mind to sleep?"

"Was counting on getting a room at Ma Laughlin's," the Kid drawled. "Can I leave my gear here until I've seen her?"

"Time you can't ain't likely to come. Put it in the office," Milt answered and, studying the state of the other's clothes, went on, "You look like you've been doing some sage-henning[1] recent."

"Why sure," the Kid agreed, having already anticipated such a question and thought up an acceptable answer. "Happen I'd called in at Watson Weller's, or some other place on my way down here, I might have been given a telegraph message saying I was wanted back at the spread."

"That's sneaky," Milt pointed out with a grin.

"Don't you-all go telling me you never did nothing like that when you rode with the Texas Light Cavalry against Santa Anna," the Kid challenged.

"Hey, Milt," the man called, before any denial could be made. "I've done. Can I get going? There's that whing-ding across town and I'd like to see what's doing."

"You might's well," Milt confirmed and, as the man

1. Sage-henning: sleeping in the open.

slouched out, continued, "For all the work he does, it wouldn't be much worse if he never came. I'll fetch you some water, hay 'n' oats."

"Gracias," the Kid answered, conscious of the honor which was being done him. Usually the hostler would have had to be asked to render such assistance. "I won't be sorry to get a bath and changed into some clean clothes."

While attending to the Appaloosa's welfare, the Kid continued to talk with Milt. Hostlers ran barbers a close second in willingness to gossip, and the old timer was no exception. However, although he commented upon the way the town had been behaving during the Bexar County Fair and the number of strangers who were attending it, he did not give any useful information. Nor did he mention, as he was sure to have done if it had happened, that anybody had been making inquiries about the possibility of the floating outfit arriving.

With his mount settled in, the Kid was free to see to his own needs. First, however, he carried his saddle and bridle into the office annex. Setting the former upon the inverted V-shaped "burro," he slid the Winchester from the boot but left the bed roll fastened to the cantle. He knew that he could do so in safety and without fear of anybody trying to interfere with it. Although he was carrying the two letters in a pouch built into the inside of his gunbelt, he was not expecting to need them that night. Not only was Guillemot unlikely to be in town until the following day, he had some other business to which he hoped to attend.

"You can allus come and bed down in the hay loft, happen Ma's got the good luck to be full up," Milt offered as the Kid headed for the main entrance.

"I'll take you up on it," the Kid promised.

Strolling leisurely in the direction of the small rooming house owned by Ma Laughlin, the Kid was as alert as always. He was soon passing through the business area of the poorer white section of the town. Although a few of the establishments were still open, he appeared to have the street to himself. That did not surprise or disturb him unduly. Commenting upon the unshaven man's eagerness to depart while helping to care for the Appaloosa, Milt had said that some of the local ranchers were throwing a barbecue to which everybody who wished to attend had been invited.

Carrying the Winchester across the crook of his left arm once more, the youngster was as prepared to bring it into action swiftly as he had been while riding towards the twin outcrops. His right hand moved on to the wrist of the butt as a figure emerged from the alley that he was approaching. Both the building which he was passing and its neighbor beyond the alley were closed and in darkness. However, there was sufficient light from the windows and open door of a store across the street for him to decide that the person in front of him was a middle-sized, plumpish woman clothed in a respectable fashion.

Even as the Kid relaxed and took his right hand away from the weapon, the woman appeared to stub her toe against an uneven board of the sidewalk. Whatever the cause, she stumbled and went down on to her bent right knee almost at his feet.

"Here, ma'am," the Kid said, bending forward and extending his right hand. "Let me help you."

The attack came so unexpectedly and fast that not even the Kid's Comanche-trained and lightning-sharp reflexes could save him from it.

Giving no outward indication of her intentions, probably because she kept her head bent forward and did not look up, the woman reached with both hands as if intending to accept the youngster's offer. Instead, she clasped hold of his wrist with a surprisingly strong grip. Surging upright as she gave a sudden and powerful tug at the trapped limb, she caught the Kid off balance. What was more, from the deft way in which she thrust her right foot between his legs to complete the ruin of his equilibrium, she must have pulled a similar trick on more than one occasion.

Unable to save himself, even though he dropped the Winchester so as to try and catch hold of the hitching rail with his left hand, the Kid reeled forward. He was already resigned to sprawling face down as he passed the end of the building. Although he saw the lurking and—under the circumstances—menacing shape in the alley from the corner of his eye, he knew that he could do nothing to protect himself.

Hissing through the air in an arc, the wicked, leather-wrapped sap in the waiting man's hand struck the Kid on the head. His Stetson robbed the blow of some of its force, but he was still pitched forward into what appeared to be a pool of brightly flashing light. As everything seemed to be swirling around him and he crashed on to the boards of the sidewalk, he heard his assailants talking.

"Are you sure he's the right one, Slippers?" demanded a harsh male voice.

"That dirty old bastard from the livery barn said it was," was the answer in tones which, although somewhat effeminate, were also masculine. "Drag him into the alley, Vern. I'll bring his rifle."

Even as the blackness started closing in about the Kid, he felt his wrists grasped and the man called "Vern" carried out the "woman's" instructions.

"Is he dead?" Slippers asked, the words coming faintly to the Kid as the dragging motion ended.

"If he ain't, I'll soon change it," Vern promised.

"No!" Slippers contradicted sharply. "Don't kill him just yet. If he doesn't have a letter, we'll need to find out how he's going to identify himself to the Ox."

Although the Kid could still hear the words, he could not attempt to struggle. Then, before Vern could reply, he slipped into unconsciousness.

Crouching over their victim's supine and motionless body, the two men started to go through his pockets. So engrossed were they in their task that neither of them saw the slender, somewhat boyish figure which was approaching from the rear end of the alley. Although armed with nothing more than what appeared to be a slender stick about eighteen inches in length, the newcomer made no attempt to raise the alarm.

"There's nothing in his pockets," Slippers complained, sounding aggrieved by the Kid's lack of consideration.

"Ain't got no money-belt on neither," Vern went on. "We'd best take him some place where we can make him answer some questions."

"Come on the—" Slippers began, the words ending as he heard a slight sound from farther along the alley. His head swung around and, seeing the slender shape, he started to straighten up, saying, "What do—?"

Once again, Slippers failed to complete a sentence. Darting closer, the newcomer brought up a kick which propelled the toe of a riding boot towards the effeminate man's jaw. Slender and boyish the figure might look to be, but there was considerable strength in its leg. So much so that Slippers might have counted himself fortunate he did not receive its full power. As it was, the foot caught him in the chest with sufficient force to lift him erect. The padding which he was wearing in that region as an aid to his disguise saved him from what would otherwise have been a painful injury. Even so, he was sent reeling bakcwards from the alley and across the sidewalk. Letting out a screech which was almost in keeping with his feminine attire, he fell from there to land rump-first on the hard-packed, wheel-rutted surface of the street.

Letting out a snarl of anger, Vern lurched upright. For a big, bulky man, he could move with a fair amount of speed. He had returned the sap to his jacket's pocket after striking the Kid down, but did not take the time to draw it. Nor did he anticipate the need for such an aid to deal with what he took to be a slim and very imprudent youth.

Thrusting out his right hand, Vern caught hold of the newcomer. He felt his fingers grasping the material of a jacket's lapel and what appeared to be a fancy, frilly-bosomed shirt such as professional gamblers frequently wore; except that it was a darker color than the usual white. Then he became aware that beneath the garments was a protuberance which ought not to have been present on a *boy*. What was more, unlike the material with which Slippers had produced his "bust," the mound was flesh and blood.

Almost as soon as the realization that he was holding a woman's left breast impacted itself on Vern's mind, causing him to slacken his grip involuntarily and to hold back the punch which he had been on the point of launching with his left fist, his captive responded in a very effective manner. Crouching slightly, she plucked herself from his grasp before he could tighten it again and pivoted her torso to the left. Reversing its direction, she drove back her bent left arm so that its elbow rammed hard into his *solar plexus*.

Taken unawares, Vern expelled all the breath from his lungs
in an agonized croaking gasp and stumbled back a few steps.
Then, spluttering what were meant to be curses, he stabbed his
right hand beneath the left side of his jacket. It emerged enfolding the bird-head butt of the nickel-plated Colt Cloverleaf
House Pistol—a four-shot revolver despite its trade name—
which had been thrust into his trousers' waistband. Cocking
back the hammer as the weapon came clear, he curled his
forefinger across the exposed trigger.

Taking warning from Vern's actions, the girl came towards
him swiftly. Her right hand, holding the thing like a short piece
of stick, swung across and upwards. Then it whipped around
and down at a somewhat gentler angle. There was a vicious
whistling sound and, although the "stick" seemed to be an
inadequate weapon, something which had the solidity of a steel
ball struck the man on the tip of his right clavicle. A sudden
shattering pan tore through him, causing him to snatch at the
Cloverleaf's trigger which had emerged from its protective
sheath when the action was cocked. Although the revolver
fired, its three-and-a-half-inch-long barrel was pointing away
from the girl. Flying above Slippers' head as he was starting
to rise, the bullet smashed through the window of the store
across the street.

Vern's Cloverleaf slipped from his numb and inoperative
fingers as his hand fell limply to his side, but he found that his
troubles had not ended. Halting, the girl swivelled with the
grace, speed and agility of a ballet dancer. The kick which she
delivered caught him in the ribs and sent him reeling towards
the mouth of the alley.

Coming to his feet, wild with fury over the attack upon him,
Slippers heard shouts from behind him and saw his companion
stumbling into view. There was, he realized, only one thing
they could do under the circumstances.

"Run, Vern!" Slippers screeched, hitching up his skirts and
starting to sprint along the street.

Clutching at his torment-spitting shoulder, the burly man
saw the wisdom of his companion's advice. The occupants of
the store were sure to come out to investigate the cause of the
shooting. In fact, even as he swung on his heel to dash after

Slippers, the first of them appeared at the doorway of the building.

Instead of following the two men whom she had attacked, the girl glanced at the Kid. He was already groaning his way back to consciousness. Satisfied that the sound would attract the attention of the men who were coming from the store, she turned and hurried silently back in the direction from which she had appeared.

Although one of the trio to leave the store was a deputy town marshal who held a revolver, he did not fire. Before he could draw a bead on either of the fleeing pair, they had darted down an alley and out of his range of vision.

"That feller come from across the street," the storekeeper announced. "Hey! Somebody's lying in there!"

Half an hour later, suffering from a headache, the Ysabel Kid was welcomed by Ma Laughlin and told that he could have a small room on the ground floor and at the rear of the building. Accepting, he asked if he could take a bath.

"I was going to insist on it," the plump, motherly woman declared, "And I'll have young Mick fix it."

On entering the bathroom, the Kid waited until Ma's grandson had filled the bathtub with hot water.

"You do something for me, *amigo?*" the Kid inquired.

"You can count on it *Cuchilo,*" Mick answered, using the Kid's Comanche man-name which meant "Knife" and had been granted in tribute to his skilled use of one.

"I want you to go to the store and fetch me two cans of kerosene."

"Is that all?"

"Nope," the Kid replied and any member of the floating outfit who had heard the gentle, almost caressing mildness of his voice would have known that it boded ill for somebody. "Happen you-all can get hold of a lil ole horned toad[2] for me, I'll pay you a dollar."

2. Horned toad: a small, short-tailed, scaly lizard of the genus *Phrynosoma* which is somewhat toad-like in appearance. The species in question would be *Phrynosoma cornutum*, The Texas Horned Lizard.

CHAPTER FIVE

It Could've Been A Sidewinder

Rosa Rio was in a fairly contented frame of mind as she crossed the passage to her private quarters on the ground floor at the rear of her *cantina*. Business had been very good that evening. With so many visitors in town, the petty thieves had been reaping a rich harvest and the majority of their plunder would eventually find its way, at far below its actual value, into her hands.

If there was one thing to spoil Rosa's sense of well-being, it was her failure to discover why Matteo Urizza had been hired and sent out of town. She always hated for something to happen without her knowledge, particularly when she sensed that it might be important and, more to the point, a source of further revenue for her.

While Rosa had put the men who hired Urizza in contact with him, receiving a good sum for her services, she had found them very reticent over what they would want him to do. Nor had she attemped to press the matter too far, knowing that to do so with them could create a bad impression and might have an adverse effect upon similar transactions in the future. Instead, she had hoped to satisfy her curiosity through other sources.

The hope had not materialized. Selected by Urizza to accompany him, young Enrique Escuchador had needed only to know that they were going to kill somebody. That was enough for him. Craving to gain a reputation of being a killer, such as his Mexican *bandido* uncle, Juan, possessed, he had been content to follow Urizza without bothering even to find out the name of their victim. Nor had Urizza's girl friend, Elena, who worked for Rosa, produced any further information. When she had attempted to raise the matter for a second time, he had given her a beating and threatened to do worse if she continued to poke her nose into his affairs.

To Rosa's way of thinking, one thing was obvious, Urizza's victim must be a person of considerable influence and consequence. Somebody whom it would be most inadvisable for him to be known to have killed. Unfortunately, she told herself as she reached towards the handle of the door to her quarters, by the time she had discovered the victim's identity, the news might be so public that she could not turn the knowledge to her financial advantage.

"Except maybe if they put a bounty on whoever did it," Rosa mused and opened the door.

The thought of betraying Urizza for such a reward brought a gold-toothed leer which made Rosa's normally unpleasant face—the passing of the years and general dissipation had ruined what, according to those who had known her in her youth, was once a great beauty—seem even more repulsive. Tall, bloatedly fat in a way that made her expensive black satin gown hang lumpily and shapeless, she was a force of evil in and around San Antonio. Yet, for all that, the town marshal and the Texas Rangers had never been able to prove her connection with, much less participation in, a single illegal activity. All that they knew for sure was that her *cantina* served as a meeting place for hired guns—especially those of mixed racial ancestry—and on occasion was visited by outlaws.

Stepping into her spacious and opulently furnished sitting-room, Rosa found it was only illuminated by the lights of the passage. Scowling angrily, she stalked towards the table in the center of the room. If the stench of kerosene which assailed her nostrils was anything to go by, her maid had filled the lamp and forgotten to light it. In fact, there was such a powerful smell from the fluid that it almost seemed the maid had been splashing it around the room.

Suddenly, for no apparent reason, the door closed. Letting out a low curse, Rosa decided that she was nearer to the table and so would light the lamp instead of returning and opening it. Even as her hands were fumbling for the box of matches, which were left on the table with the cigar humidor she kept for use by important visitors, she thought that she heard a click from behind her.

It was, Rosa thought, the sound a key would make when turned in a lock.

Yet she knew it could not be that.

While there was a key in the door, Rosa very rarely made use of it. Nobody would dare to enter without her permission, much less try to rob her.

With that comforting thought arrived at, the woman's fingers touched the matchbox and there was a faint rattling sound from its contents.

"Wouldn't go lighting no matches, was I you," said a gentle, almost mild voice. "Not with all this kerosene scattered hither and yon."

"What—!" Rosa began, so startled that she could neither say nor do anything more practical.

"And don't go yelling for help," the speaker continued. "The door's locked 'n' it'd be all hell for 'em to bust it open. On top of which, *I've* got me some matches, one of 'em ready to strike. I know where the kerosene's at—and I don't mind if I have to set your place on fire."

Recovering from her shock with commendable speed, Rosa moved slowly and as silently as she could manage around the table as the unseen speaker was delivering his warning. On reaching the place where she usually sat—facing the door—when receiving visitors, she felt for and started to ease open the drawer in which she kept a loaded and cocked twin-barrelled, ten-guage shotgun which had been cut down to little over a foot in length.

However, try as she might, the woman could not pinpoint

her unseen visitor's exact location. Obviously he must have been standing behind the door when she entered, so that he would be unseen until he had closed and locked it. Yet there was a strange ventriloquial effect—although Rosa would not have known how to express such a term—which rendered her unable to be sure whether he was still there or had moved.

"Just who the hell are you?" the woman demanded, speaking English as fluently as the visitor. However, she was far less interested in learning his identity than in discovering his exact whereabouts.

"The name's Loncey Dalton Ysabel," came the reply, but it seemed to be far from where she had last heard it.

"Loncey—!" Rosa began, then realization struck her and she felt as if she had been touched by an icy hand. She went on in Spanish, *"C-Cabrito! Is that you?"*

At one time or another, Rosa had had practically every dangerous killer or badly wanted outlaw in Texas under her roof. Yet none of them, not even Bad Bill Longley, John Wesley Hardin or the savage and murderously unpredictable Ben Thompson, had filled her with the alarm which she was now experiencing. She remembered the Ysabel Kid all too well from the days when he had ridden the smuggler trails with his father. Young as he had been, the toughest and most ornery hard-cases had grown silent and uneasy in his presence. Many had been the tales which were told about his terribly effective way of dealing with his enemies. Nor had his taking employment on the OD Connected ranch changed his ways, if all the stories that were still being circulated did not lie. Rosa was one who believed that they were true.

However, no matter what her enemies might say about her complete lack of moral scruples, Rosa Rio was no coward. So she reached into the drawer in search of the sawed-off shotgun. Once she had it in her hands, she felt confident that she could deal with even the Ysabel Kid. All she needed to know was roughly where he was standing. The weapon held nine .32 caliber buckshot balls in each barrel, and they would spread in such a manner that some at least were sure to find their mark.

With that in mind, Rosa waited anxiously for a reply to her question.

"It's me," the Kid confirmed, in just as excellent Spanish. Moving on silent feet through the darkness, he made his way towards the window which he had opened as part of his preparations for extracting information from what he had known would be a *very* reluctant source. Reverting to English, he continued, "Only, from now on, it's me's'll do the asking and you the answering."

While her unwelcome visitor's voice once again seemed to be originating from somewhere entirely different to its last position, Rosa felt sure that she had located it. At that moment, her little finger brushed against an object and she knew what it must be because there was never anything except the shotgun in the drawer.

Sucking in an anticipatory and satisfied breath, the woman grabbed for the object which she had touched.

After having taken his bath, the Kid had donned his all black clothing. However, he had replaced his boots with a pair of *Pehnane* moccasins. As most of the Kid's work entailed some form of scouting, much of which was of necessity performed on foot, he did not require the high heels that cowhands found necessary. The task which he was proposing to carry out that night was such as to require a greater silence of movement than would be permitted by his boots.

Young Mick Laughlin had produced the items which the Kid had requested, but had not been told of the purpose they were to serve. Fortunately, their conversation had been curtailed by the arrival of Town Marshal Anse Dale.

Having been told about the attack on the Kid, Dale had sensed that there might have been more than a mere attempted robbery behind it. So he had come in search of further information. Knowing the marshal to be a shrewd, honest peace officer and also a good friend of his employer, the Kid had been frank in his explanation. Without disclosing its nature, he had said that he was on Ole Devil Hardin's business and had described the partially successful ambush. Dale had always made a habit of trying to keep in touch with any happenings in San Antonio which could end in criminal activity. So he had heard from an informer that Matt Urizza had left town accompanied by Enrique Escuchador, but—until that moment—he had not known the nature of their business.

Turning to the subject of the more recent attack, Dale had drawn conclusions which had come close to matching the Kid's thoughts regarding its purpose. The two assailants had probably had more than a chance robbery in mind, for they would have been unlikely to consider the Kid a lucrative prospect as a victim. Which had implied that they had known who to look for and where to find him.

Although at that time the Kid had forgotten the conversation which he had overheard while drifting into unconsciousness, he had been able to offer an explanation as to where they had gathered their information. Only two people had known of his arrival and intentions. As he trusted the hostler, Milt, the man who had been sweeping out the livery barn was the logical suspect.

Knowing something of the Kid's forthright way of dealing with such matters, Dale had stated that he would personally find and question the man. Having had other things in mind and being satisfied that the marshal was better able to locate the man, if restricted in the methods he could use to elicit the required answer, the Kid had not argued. He had described as best he could the assailant whom he had seen, but had realized how little use the description would be as the man whould have already discarded his female attire. Promising to do all he could, but warning that finding the attackers would not be easy with so many strangers in town, Dale had taken his departure.

The time had been close to midnight when the Kid had left Ma Laughlin's rooming house. Equipped for the task which lay ahead, he had made his way to the Mexican quarter. He was not carrying his Winchester, having concluded that the bowie knife and old Dragoon Colt would be adequate for his needs and more suitable in an emergency.

Waiting for his opportunity with the patience of a *Pehnane* brave on a "raiding"[1] mission, the Kid had entered Rosa Rio's *cantina* by its rear door. He had been there on several occasions in his border-smuggling youth and had found that the interior layout was much as he had remembered it from those days. Going into the owner's private quarters, having already checked through the window that they were unoccupied, he had closed

---

1. Raiding: a polite name for the Comanche pastime of horse stealing.

the door and made ready for her arrival.

All in all, the Kid considered that everything was going as
he had planned. Finding herself in darkness, Rosa had crossed
to the table with the intention of lighting the lamp instead of
returning and opening the door. That was what he had hoped
would happen. If she had done the opposite, she would have
spoiled his arrangements and made his task more difficult.

Thinking of the surprise which she was going to hand to
the invader of her privacy, Rosa closed her fingers—

But not upon the smooth metal or wood of the sawed-off
shotgun!

Instead, her hand was enfolding something cold, scaly—

And which moved!

Feeling whatever she had taken hold of struggling in her
grasp, Rosa knew that she was most certainly *not* touching the
weapon. Considering the person with whom she was dealing,
her imagination suggested the nature of the thing which she
was gripping. That belief was given what she regarded as complete confirmation when she heard—sounding shockingly loud
under the circumstances—the patter caused by spots of liquid
striking the side of the drawer.

Like many women of her day and age, Rosa had a dread
of snakes and reptiles. The thought that she was probably grasping a deadly poisonous, venom-spitting creature completely
unnerved her.

Snatching away her hand, the woman give a screech and
staggered back until she was halted by the wall. Her whole
body was shaking with the violence of her reaction to what she
believed to have been a narrow escape from a particularly
unpleasant death.

"Don't know what you're taking on like that for, Rosa,"
came the Kid's voice, but from an entirely different region to
that in which she had estimated he would be. "It wasn't nothing
but a lil ole horned toad. I've got some pack-rat in me and I
just couldn't take that sawed-off ten gauge from the drawer
without putting something in its place. Now could I?"

Cold rage drove through the woman as she listened to the
sardonically drawled words, driving out something of the terror. She knew that such a creature as the Kid had mentioned

was completely harmless, although apt to be disconcerting due
to its habit of squirting drops of blood from the forward corners
of its eyes—for distances of up to three feet—when alarmed.

"Y-you—son-of-a-bitch!" Rosa croaked, but realized as she
spoke that she would have fired in entirely the wrong direction
if the shotgun had been available.

"Don't take it too hard," the Kid advised. "I didn't want
to do you no hurt." Then a subtly different timber crept into
his voice and he went on, "But it could've been a sidewinder
just's easy."

"What the hells's all this about, *Cabrito?*" Rosa demanded,
struggling—but not entirely succeeding—to conceal her growing sense of trepidation.

"I've been jumped twice just recently," the Kid replied,
getting down to the reason for his visit. "First time it was by
Matt Urizza and Enrique Escuchador—" He heard a low gasp
from the woman and knew that he was justified in coming to
see her. "They put lead into Dusty Fog—"

"So that's who—!" Rosa began, before she could stop herself, appreciating the reason for Urizza's reticence and knowing
that she had guessed correctly at its cause. No man in his right
mind would openly boast that he was setting off to try to kill
Dusty Fog. "Is he dead?"

"Do you reckon I'd be playing fool games with *horned toads*
happen he was?"

For all her hardness, the woman shuddered as she listened
to the gently spoken—yet, somehow, chillingly menacing—
reply.

"Nope, he was just hurt a mite," the Kid went on. "Escuchador's dead though. But Urizza got clean away. Which's a
pity, 'cause I was wanting to ask him what he'd got against
a couple of good-hearted, loving-natured lil ole Texas boys like
Dusty 'n' me."

"Wh-what do you want from me?" Rosa asked, conscious
that her voice was displaying anxiety.

"Who sent them after us?"

"I—I didn't!"

"You know who did."

"How would—?"

"This room'll be on fire happen you can't do better than that by the time I've counted five," the Kid warned. "And I'm starting at 'three.'"

"On the Holy Mother's name, *Cabrito!*" Rosa wailed, certain that she was not hearing an idle threat. "I don't know!"

"Day anybody hires a feller like Urizza in San Antonio and *you're* not in on it, I'll start to vote Republican."

"It's true, *Carbrito!*"

"Four!" said the Kid. "Fi—!"

"I don't know his name!" the woman almost shrieked. "I only saw him the once!"

"Who?" the Kid insisted remorselessly.

"This *hombre!* A dude! You know that I *never* ask for a name!" Rosa explained, spluttering the words out almost incoherently. "He said he'd got word that I could tell him where to hire a *pistolero valiente*—"

"And you admitted all honest and true that you could—to a *stranger*."

"The feller he said sent him was Ram Turtle, so I knew he was all right. Anyway, he paid me and I sent Matt Urizza over to his table."

"And then what?" the Kid prompted.

"That's all I know," Rosa replied in an almost pleading manner. "Honest to God, *Cabrito*. Sure, I knew Urizza was wanted to kill somebody, but neither of them let on who. Would *you* have, knowing *who* you was after?"

"I'm not real likely to be fool enough to go after Dusty, much less *me*," the Kid pointed out, sensing that he was being told the truth. He also conceded that Urizza would be unlikely to make public names of such victims as he had been hired to kill. "What's this *hombre* look like?"

"Big, thickset, wore range clothes with a hat so big it hid his hair and had got a false black beard," the woman answered. "He wasn't no Texan, sounded German or some such."

"You'd want to know more about him than that, even if he did come with Ram Turtle's backing," the Kid stated. "Where's he staying at in town?"

"I only wish I knew!" Rosa declared bitterly and almost indignantly. "The sneaky son-of-a-bitch must've guessed I'd have him followed. He bust the skull of the boy I sent afore

they was out of the Mexican quarter. So I don't know where
he is, or even if he's still in town."

"He could be," the kid drawled, thinking of the second
attack.

Neither of the speakers' voices had been Germanic in accent
or timber but the man who had struck the Kid down had conveyed an impression of possessing size and bulk. Anybody
smart enough to disguise his appearance would also be likely
to change the manner in which he normally spoke.

"Where's Urizza now?" the Kid inquired, keeping his summation to himself.

"I've not heard about it if he's come back," Rosa answered.

"Happen you see him," the Kid requested, "tell him I said,
'Ahi te huacho.'"[2]

"I'll do that," the woman promised, guessing the meeting
was coming to an end and, boiling with anger at the way she
had been treated, starting to consider how to take her revenge
upon her unasked and unwanted visitor.

"One thing, though," the Kid's voice cut in, and Rosa for
the first time felt sure that it was coming from several feet
away, near the window, "Happen you've got any notions about
trying to get even with me for coming calling all uninvited this
way, I wouldn't do it was I you. If I get just the teensiest call
to think you have, there's going to be word passing 'round that
somebody told Dusty 'n' me how Urizza 'n' Enrique Escuchador was gunning for us, which's how we knowed and poor ole
Enrique got made wolf-bait. Why his Uncle Juan might even
figure's it was you's done it. 'Specially as I'll have said it
was."

"You bastard!" the woman spat out, being able to foresee
the possible consequences of such a rumor. Juan Eschuchador
would feel compelled to take revenge upon whoever was responsible for his nephew's death. However, she was not over-
perturbed about it, having considerable strength of backing if
he should come looking for trouble.

"Happen that don't make you see reason," the Kid continued, apparently from the same place. "Make good and sure
whoever you send kills me as dead as a six-day stunk-up skunk.

2. *Ahi te huacho:* colloquial Mexican-Spanish term meaning, "I'll be watching for you."

'Cause if he doesn't, you'll never dare to go out of doors, nor even sleep at night, for wondering when I'll be coming to pay you back. No matter what you'd do, nor how many men you had around, one night you'd feel my hand on you—Like this!''

Listening to the quiet, menacing speech, Rosa had no idea that the speaker was drawing closer. Yet, with a final exclamation, a hand pressed on her shoulder. Letting out a squawk of terror, she sprang away. Stumbling on to a chair, which collapsed under her weight, she was precipitated to the floor and winded by her landing. By the time she had recovered her breath, the Kid had gone.

Rising, Rosa fumbled her way unsteadily to the table. With shaking hands, she found the matches and lit the lamp. As she stared around the room, she could not hold back a shudder. There were several heaps of kerosene-soddened paper on the floor and the shotgun was half buried in one of them. Sinking into her chair, she glanced into the open drawer. The horned lizard had apparently climbed out, but the spots of blood it had ejected showed plainly on the wood. Shivering involuntarily, she reached a conclusion. No real harm had been done. Even her dignity would not suffer if she made no mention of the visit. So, having no desire to engage in a feud with the Kid, she decided to forget her plans for trying to take revenge upon him.

CHAPTER SIX

The Most Dangerous Man In Europe

Although the Ysabel Kid believed that he would have no further need for concern over Rosa Rio's objections to his visit, especially so soon and after the fright he had given her, he maintained his usual wary vigilance as he walked back towards Ma Laughlin's rooming house. He was satisfied that the woman had had neither part in organizing nor knowledge of the second attack, which indicated that somebody else might be after the bounty on his scalp. He still did not know how, or why, his assailants had been driven off; except that he had had nothing to do with it. Whatever the reason had been they were still at liberty and might even now be searching for him in the hope of having another stab at earning their pay. If *that* happened, their next attempt could be made with guns.

For all the Kid's thoughts on the subject, he came into sight of Ma Laughlin's without having had need for his constant alertness. However, despite the comforting feeling that he would shortly be climbing through the window into his room—

having left through it when setting off to visit Rosa Rio, so as to have an alibi if necessary—he did not relax.

Which proved to be fortunate.

Stepping over the picket fence, the Kid moved quietly across Ma Laughlin's truck garden towards the window. Even as his hands went towards it, he realized that something was different from when he had taken his departure.

The window was fully closed!

Yet he had left it open just enough to be able to insert his fingers to facilitate his return!

Even in the unlikely event of Ma, or her grandson, entering and discovering that their guest was absent, they would not have touched anything.

Nor was it likely that the window had slipped into the closed position during his absence.

All of which added up to one thing, to the Kid's way of thinking.

Some unauthorized person had arrived after his departure, entered the room and was now awaiting his return.

Scowling, the Kid gave very rapid consideration to what he should do. One thing was instantly apparent. He could not stand for any length of time thinking about the matter. If he did, whoever was in the room would become suspicious and realize that his—or their—presence had been detected.

Bearing that aspect in mind, the Kid reached his decision. While his left hand began to ease the window open, his right turned palm outwards to enfold the worn walnut grips of the old Colt Dragoon. He would have preferred to use his bowie knife, so as to avoid disturbing the whole household, but he might have been observed as he reached across to extract it.

"Ma's going to be riled's all hell happen there's shooting." the Kid mused as he curled his thumb across the Dragoon's hammer-spur and prepared to twist it from its holster. "How the hell do I get into things like this?"

"I didn't know that the Ox had arrived yet, Lon," announced a gentle, well-educated Southron woman's voice which the youngster recognized even as he had started to move aside and clear of the window. "What did you make of him?"

"Belle!" the Kid ejaculated, too amazed to offer an answer. Coming to a halt, he allowed the half-drawn Colt to slip back into its holster and went on, *"Belle Boyd! Well I'll be damned!"*

"According to Betty Hardin, who should know, there's nothing more likely than that," replied the woman in the room and her voice was bubbling with suppressed laughter. "Come on in and close the drapes so that I can light the lamp and we'll have ourselves a talk."

Shaking his head in bewilderment, the Kid did as his as yet unseen visitor requested. Climbing through the window, he closed it and pulled the drapes together. A match rasped and the stench caused by its phosphorus and sulphur head igniting came to his nostrils as the lamp was being lit. Turning, he looked across the room.

Standing by the small dressing table, the young woman was about five foot seven in height, slender—but far from skinny—with black hair that was cropped almost boyishly short and a very beautiful face. She had on a black, two-piece tailored costume of the current severe cut and lines that still emphasized her shapely figure. The jacket covered a dark blue blouse with a frilly bosom and a man's black bow-tie. The flared skirt was long, although it did not hide the toes of what the Kid guessed would be a pair of serviceable riding boots. On the bed, alongside a closed parasol, lay a dainty "jockey" hat which was pinned to a wig of fashionably-styled blonde curls.

"Surprised to see me, Lon?" the girl inquired, with a smile.

"Oh *no!*" the Kid replied. "I allus expect to find you in my room after midnight. It happens so often, I can't rightly get to sleep the times you're not there."

"I saw *you* earlier tonight," Belle said, shaking hands and still showing amusement at his perplexity. "But you were in what Betty says is your usual state."

"What might *that* be?"

"Sleeping."

"Sleeping?" the Kid repeated, wishing that he could stop sounding so puzzled. Then he remembered what he had been told about the attack. The deputy had suggested that he had been fighting with his assailants until he had been clubbed down and they fled, which he had known all along was impossible. At last he knew the real explanation. "So you cut in, huh?"

"Betty will never forgive me," Belle answered, sitting on

the end of the bed. "But I have to confess that I cut in."

That a slender girl would even consider trying to defend him by physical means against two men did not surprise the Kid. Not when she was Belle Boyd; who had won the name the Rebel Spy during the War Between The States and now worked as an agent for the United States' Secret Service.[1] With her somewhat unconventional unbringing,[2] she was well able to defend herself.

"And started to whomping them evil-doers with your lil ole parasol's handle, huh?" the Kid suggested.

Nor was the comment made in a facetious manner. He knew that, telescoped into the detachable handle, the parasol concealed a powerful coil-spring billy with a round steel ball for its head.

"I kicked Slippers where it would really have hurt him if he'd been a woman instead of only dressed like one, although I was aiming at his head," Belle corrected. "I admit I did take a swing at Vernet, but I only got him on the top of the shoulder."

"Sounds like you know them," the Kid commented.

"I do. They work for Roger de Leclerc."

"Who'd this-here de Leclerc *hombre* be?"

"Although he'd hate for you to call him anything so crude, he's France's best spy," Belle replied.

"Happen he set them two jaspers to abusing me that ways, I'll call him something a whole heap cruder 'n' that," the Kid declared. "And then I'll ask him real polite-like why he done it. 'S far's I know, I've never done nothing to give a French spy cause to be riled at me. I've never even called him one."

"He may have wanted to stop you meeting the Ox," Belle suggested.

"Who-all's this-here 'Ox' *hombre* you keep talking ab—" the Kid began, then remembrance flooded back. "Hell's fire! One of them jaspers said something about wanting to find out how I was going to identify myself to the Ox. I've never heard of any such feller."

"He's the most dangerous man in Europe," Belle said soberly. "Or was. Right now he's in the good old U.S. of A. and

1. How this came about is told in: *Back to the Bloody Border*.
2. Details of Belle Boyd's history and qualifications are given in Appendix 3.

coming to San Antonio to meet you. His full name is Octavius Xavier Guillemot."

"Octavius Xavier Guillemot!" the Kid spat the words out. "But he's—"

"Yes," Belle interrupted. "He's the man who you're going to take into Mexico so that he can ask Don Arsenio Serrano to give back James Bowie's knife."

"Nope," the Kid corrected. "After what you've just told me, he's the *hombre* I'm *not* going to take."

"Why not?"

"Ole Devil said we should do it for Resin Bowie's man. Which, according to you, this 'Ox' *hombre's* not all that likely to be."

"I'd still like you to go, Lon," Belle requested. "And to take me with you if we can find a way to do it."

"I don't follow your trail," the Kid declared.

"It's like this," the girl elaborated. "General Handiman is *very* interested in learning why the Ox is going to all this trouble to obtain Bowie's knife."

"He can likely sell it for over a thousand dollars," the Kid suggested, knowing that the officer mentioned by Belle was the head of the United States' Secret Service.

"A thousand dollars would hardly cover his expenses. And he wouldn't look at any deal unless there was well over fifty thousand dollars clear profit in it for him. He's the biggest of the international criminals and I don't just mean his size."

"If he's such an all-fired big owlhoot, how come he's roaming around on the hoof and not in a hoosegow some place?"

"Why weren't you and your father ever put in jail?" Belle countered.

"We was never caught doing anything wrong," the Kid replied.

"The same applies to the Ox," Belle told him. "Every police force and Secret Service in Europe knows about him, but they've never been able to prove a thing."

"Could be that's 'cause he's never done nothing 'cept make out he had," the Kid drawled, crossing to sit with his rump hooked on the corner of the dressing-table. "I knowed a feller like that once. Allus telling about how he'd ridden with owl-hoots. Only he'd never done no such thing."

"The Ox has done plenty," Belle stated. "And most of the Secret Services could prove it, because they've all used him, or bought things from him which they knew he didn't own and had no right to be selling."

"Including you-all?" asked the Kid.

"Anyway," Belle went on, neither confirming nor denying the question. "The General was very interested when he heard that the Ox was over here. I can't tell you how, but we found out that he'd gone to see Resin Bowie, the Second, then contacted General Hardin to ask for help in collecting the original bowie knife from Don Arsenio Serrano. What we're just dying to know is, why does he want it? The French and the Germans want to know, too."

"I hear tell that them French and Germans don't get on too well," the Kid remarked quietly.

"The war between them ended back in seventy-one," Belle replied, studying the young Texan's Indian-dark features in a speculative manner. "But I wouldn't say that they're friendly."

"So they'd not be likely to team up together to find out what's going on?"

"From what I've heard about Leclerc and Horst von Uhlmann, I'd think it would be most *unlikely*. Why do you ask?"

The Kid told Belle of the ambush and its aftermath, assuring her that Dusty Fog had suffered only comparatively minor injuries even though they had been sufficient to prevent him continuing with the assignment. Then he he went on to give her the information which he had extracted from Rosa Rio, without offering to explain the means he had used to acquire it. Nor did she ask. After her inquiry about the small Texan's condition, the girl listened without interrupting.

"I didn't realize that the Germans were here already," Belle remarked at the end of the Kid's story.

"Huh?"

"I thought I was here ahead of them all until I saw Slippers and Vernet this evening. But I suppose one of the Germans could have made even better time than I did."

"How'd they know where to come?"

"Perhaps the same way that I did," Belle answered. "Or they could have had another source of information. I've been doing this kind of work for too long to be surprised over learning that other people have found out as much as I have."

"Do you reckon one of them French jaspers pretended to be a German while he was hiring Urizza so, happen there was trouble, they'd get blamed?"

"It's possible. Vernet would fit the description. But, according to the register at the Henry Hotel, they only took their room there this morning. Which, before you tell me, doesn't mean that they couldn't have been in town earlier."

"I never said a word," the Kid protested. "Hey though! How come you was on hand and didn't do nothing until *after* they'd whomped me on my poor lil ole head?"

"I thought Betty would prefer it that way," Belle replied with a smile, then became serious. "I'd seen them leaving their hotel and was following them hoping to learn what their game was. But I was too far away to hear what the man from the livery barn was telling them. And I couldn't chance going closer while they were waiting in the alley. Of course, I assumed that they were waiting for *somebody* and might have guessed who it was if I'd known then who the man from the livery barn was. By the time I found out it was you, it was too late to do anything except stop them doing anything worse to you."

"Why'n't you stick around after they'd lit out?"

"I wasn't dressed for it," Belle answered. "If I'd been seen without my skirt, it would aroused the kind of attention I want to avoid. So, as soon as I saw that you'd be looked after, I dressed and went to find Slippers and Vernet."

"Did you do it?" the Kid asked and something in his gentle words brought the girl's eyes to his face.

"Yes," Belle said flatly.

"Where're they at?" demanded the Kid and it was all of that, despite his gentle tones.

"Back at their room," Bell replied.

"Are they now?" the Kid drawled, looking as innocent as a fresh-scrubbed choir-boy, as his right hand drifted towards the hilt of the bowie knife. "I reckon I'll sort of drift along and say 'howdy.'"

"Call it evens, Lon," Belle requested.

"Call it *evens!*" the Kid snorted indignantly. "After they whomped me on the head 'n'—"

"I think I broke Vernet's collar-bone," Belle interrupted. "They sent for a doctor as soon as they got back to the hotel. I'd say that's a fair trade for an itty-bitty tap on the head. It wasn't as if they hit you anywhere they could've damaged."

"I'll let *that* pass," the Kid growled. "Only they could've sent Urizza after us, which's another thing entirely."

"They *could* have," Belle conceded. "But, if they did, they weren't showing much faith in him."

"How come?"

"They had a man watching out for whoever came from the OD Connected at the livery barn," the girl pointed out.

"Just to make sure we didn't get by Urizza," the Kid countered.

"I'm not gainsaying it," Belle assured him. "All I want you to do is let it ride, at least until we know who-all else's in the deal."

"You mean there might be more of 'em?"

"If France and Germany are interested, it's possible the English are too and other European countries."

"Damn it all!" the Kid grunted. "You mean all of them countries might be wanting to lay hands on ole Jim Bowie's knife?"

"If that's what the Ox is really after," Belle agreed.

"But you said he wasn't likely to go after something unless it's real valuable," the Kid reminded her.

"I did," Belle admitted. "And that's why I've been sent to find out what he's after. Will you stay clear of Slippers and Vernet for the time being, Lon?"

"Going after 'em could make fuss for you, huh?"

"It won't make things any easier. How about it?"

"I was hoping you'd talk me out of going," the Kid declared, rising and unbuckling his gunbelt. Placing it on the chair by the bed, he went on, "Hey though, how did you know where to find me."

"That was easy," Belle replied. "I just came here—"

"Why *here?*" the Kid wanted to know.

"Because I remembered when I was on vacation at the OD Connected, one of you said that you all always stayed here when you came to San Antonio," Belle explained. "So I came to see Ma as soon as I arrived and was lucky enough to get the next to last empty room. Nobody had taken the other when I left this evening, but it was occupied when I came back."

"Why didn't you come and see me——?" the Kid began.

"I did, except that, due to trying to find the man from the livery barn and all, it was gone midnight when I arrived. I wasn't absolutely sure it was you in the room, so I came around the back to find out. The window was open a little and the room deserted, but your rifle, saddle and bed roll were in it. So I decided that you'd gone out to look for the Ox and, with you being away for so long, that he'd arrived. In fact, I was just thinking about coming to try to find you when you returned."

"I was like to come in shooting when I figured there was somebody in here," the Kid warned.

"And I was all set to shoot, if it hadn't been you," Belle countered, lifting her hat and wig to show that they had been concealing a pearl-handled, nickel-plated Remington Double Derringer. Then she gestured towards his gunbelt. "May I?"

"Feel free," the Kid assented.

"James Black made this, didn't he?" Belle asked, having drawn the knife from its sheath.

"Why sure," the Kid agreed. "It's modeled exactly on Jim Bowie's."[3]

"It's excellently made," the girl commented, turning the weapon over in her hands, then tapping the blade with her left thumbnail.

"They do say old James Black made the best steel in these United States," the Kid replied. "And he did even better than his best when he whomped up that toad-sticker for Jim Bowie."

"In what way?"

"Story is that Jim Bowie took him along a carved-out wooden model and asked him to copy it with the best steel he knew how to make——"

"Of course!" Belle interrupted. "The legend is that James Black made the steel by melting down a piece of a star that had fallen near to his forge."[4]

3. Although the Kid did not know it, his knife—having an eleven and a half inch long, two and a half inch wide, blade—was slightly larger than Bowie's original model.

4. Further details of this legend are given in Paul I. Wellman's: *The Iron Mistress*.

"So I've always heard," the Kid agreed. "And they do say that the blade it made was so tough 'n' sharp that it'd cut through any other knife—Hey! Maybe that's why all these jaspers want to get hold of it."

"How do you mean?"

"Happen the steel's that good, it'd sure hell be worth a heap of money anybody's knowed how to make it."

"There's only one thing wrong with that," Belle objected, returning the Kid's weapon to its sheath. "If the legend is true and the knife was made from a piece of a star, there wouldn't be any way that the steel could be duplicated. Unless, of course, you had a whole lot more pieces."

CHAPTER SEVEN

A Mistake Like *That* Could Get You Shot

"Mr. *Octavius Xavier* Guillemot—*sir?*" asked the plump, pompous-looking clerk at the Sandford Hotel, lifting his gaze from the brass-framed Winchester Model of 1866 rifle which had been placed on the well-polished top of the reception desk and glancing uneasily at its owner. The final honorific had clearly been an after-thought.

Although the black-dressed cowhand—or so the clerk, having only recently arrived in the West, assumed the Ysabel Kid to be—had appeared very young and unsure of himself as he had stepped into the opulent lobby of San Antonio de Bexar's most luxurious hotel, a closer inspection had left its doubts. The clerk had been on the point of delivering a sharp protest when the rifle had been laid in front of him, and the words had gone unuttered. There was a sardonic glint, almost a mocking challenge, in the newcomer's red hazel eyes which the clerk had found disconcerting and even unnerving. The glint had suggested that he should not attempt to be too high-handed.

63

However, being conscious of the dignity of his position, the clerk had tried to throw off the sensation. His querying of the name given by the "cowhand" had been a vain attempt to re-establish the correct relationship between them. Even as he had started to do so, he had been wondering if an insistence on social standing was a good idea in this case.

"There's not *real* likely to be more than one gent name of 'Guillemot' staying here, even in a fancy, high-toned place like this, now is there?" challenged the Kid, who was rarely influenced by atmosphere and impervious to unwarranted disapproval. "I mean, they're not running around all over the range like 'Smiths,' 'Joneses' or 'Rileys.'"

"Is Mr. Guillemot expecting you, sir?" the clerk asked stiffly.

"I reckon he just might be."

"May I inquire your name?"

"It wouldn't do no good, even if I told you," the Kid declared "But General Hardin sent me."

"From the OD Connected ranch, sir?" the clerk inquired and there was a slight change in his attitude.

"Like you said," the Kid drawled. "From the OD Connected ranch."

"I see," the clerk said, glancing at the rifle and returning his gaze to the center of the Kid's chest. He could not meet the coldly mocking scrutiny of the red-hazel eyes. "Mr. Guillemot is in Room Twenty-One, sir. I'll have a boy show you up."

"Shucks, I found my way from the spread to here without having no 'boy' lead me by the hand," the Kid protested, picking up his rifle. "I reckon I might just about make it the rest of the way."

"It—It's the rule of the establishment, sir," the clerk said nervously.

"Wouldn't want to go busting no rules in a fancy place like this," the Kid stated, watching the flicker of relief cross the man's sallow features as he rang the bell on the desk and a boy wearing a bellhop's livery came forward. "Howdy, *amigo*. Looks like you're my scout over this-here trail."

"Number Twenty-One," the clerk ordered, glaring at the grinning and apparently unimpressed boy. As he watched them walking away, he took out a handkerchief and mopped daintily at his brow, thinking, "I should never have left Baltimore. People knew their place there."

Oblivious of the clerk's sentiments, which would not have worried him even if he had been aware of them, the Kid accompanied the youngster upstairs. He was conscious of the way in which the bellhop was studying him, with particular attention to his clothes and armament.

"Hey," the boy said, having scrutinized the Winchester and Dragoon Colt. "Aren't you the Ysabel Kid?"

"Don't you go telling anybody," the Kid replied, knowing that he would obtain information by admitting the truth. "But I am."

"Wowee!" the boy breathed. "Wait until I tell the other fellers about *this!*"

"What's this gent I'm going to see like, *amigo?*" the Kid inquired.

"He's a dude," the boy replied, but his voice did not hold the kind of contempt which would normally have accompanied such a term. "A hard cuss, 'less I miss my guess. Walks 'n' talks like a bow-necked Army officer, but he could be a Pink Eye."

"Huh huh," the Kid grunted, comparing the information with Belle Boyd's description of Guillemot the previous night. Although they had not come any closer to solving the mystery, they had formulated a plan which might help them do so before she had returned to her own room. He was on his way to put the first stage of the plan into operation. "What makes you reckon that?"

"He's got that big *hombre* who's been hanging around all week up there with him."

"Which big *hombre?*"

"He's another dude. A big square-head. Got papers saying he's a Pink-Eye's 's been sent down here to keep watch for owlhoots's might've come in for the County Fair."

Although nothing showed on his Indian-dark features, the Kid found the bellhop's information very interesting. It was, he realized, possible—even probable—that the Pinkerton National Detective Agency might send their "Pink-Eye" operatives to San Antonio to keep watch for wanted men or known criminals, particularly any with sufficient money to stay at the Sandford Hotel. They might even have heard of Guillemot's intention to visit the town and hoped to achieve what the official law enforcement organizations of the world had failed to do, catch him committing a crime. Or somebody might have hired them to try to find out what had brought him from Eruope. It was even possible that he had hired them to watch out for his various enemies.

However, the term "square-head" was applied to men of Teutonic nationality. All came under the same ethnic classification in the Old West, whether they be Danish, Dutch, Norwegian, Swedish—or German!

According to the bellhop, the "square-head" had been in town for at least a week. Which meant that he could have been the man who had hired Urizza.

There was no time for the Kid to consider the matter too extensively. They were already approaching the door marked "21".

"Say one thing," the boy went on, oblivious of the disturbing possibilities his news had produced for the Kid. "Them Pink-Eyes sure live well. This-here suite's the best in the house."

Before any more could be said, the bellhop knocked on the door.

"Come in!" called a hard, commanding voice.

"Means you, not me," the boy remarked. "Said for me to fetch whoever come up and let 'em go in.

Opening the door, after tipping the boy and watching him scuttle away, the Kid entered. He was carrying the Winchester in his right hand as he walked in and looked around. There was a door at either side, giving access to the rest of the suite. The one at the left was slightly ajar. Noticing that, while closing the door behind him, he turned his attention to the occupants of the sitting room.

One, standing by the window, was a tall, lean, hard-looking man with close-cropped brown hair and clad in expensive Eastern riding clothes. There was, as the boy had said, something of a military air about him. It was the look of a hard martinet officer, which the smile on his face did little to soften.

Seated at the table, the second occupant of the room came as a surprise to the Kid. Brown haired, dressed in a dark-grey two-piece traveling costume which set off a richly endowed figure, the beautiful young woman met his gaze. However, she neither moved nor spoke.

"You have come from General Hardin?" the man asked, speaking English with an accent which the Kid could not identify.

"Why sure," the youngster replied, taking his gaze from the woman.

"I'm pleased to meet you," the man stated, extending his right hand. He did not, however, offer to advance.

"Same with me," the Kid drawled, transferring the Winchester to his left hand as he took his first step forward. Flickering another glance at the young woman, he noticed that she gave what might have been a quick, but definite negative shake of her head. Walking across the room in a very leisurely fashion, he allowed the Winchester to slide until he held it at the wrist of the butt and with the muzzle pointing at the floor. At the same time, he continued speaking in a matter-of-fact manner. "Know a feller name of 'Limping Joe' who allus used to squeeze 'stead of just shaking hands. Just for a joke, 'cept he hurt, way he did it. Only one time he started squeezing when t'other feller was holding a rifle and the feller couldn't stop his-self pulling the trigger. Which's why they call him '*Limping Joe*.'"

So well had the Kid coordinated his words and movements that his story came to an end just before he reached the other man. However, he glanced downwards as he thrust forward his right hand.

The man's eyes followed the direction in which the Kid was looking, then snapped up to stare hard at his face. The quick examination had disclosed that the muzzle of the Winchester was almost touching the center of his well-polished brown Hessian-type riding boot. More significantly, not only was the rifle's hammer at the fully cocked position, the youngster's little, third and second fingers were inside the loading lever's ring while his forefinger was curled over the trigger. Nobody who had any experience with firearms—which Ole Devil Hardin's representative was certain to possess—would commit such a blunder unintentionally. Although nothing in his visitor's guileless young face gave any inkling of whatever thoughts might lie beyond it, the man swung his head momentarily towards the partially open door and shook it in an urgently prohibitive manner.

"So *you're* Mr. Guillemot," the Kid drawled, in an amiable tone which gave no indication of his true feelings. Then, without actually looking at the young woman, he jerked his head in her direction and went on, "And this'll be Mrs. Guillemot, I reckon."

Although the Kid had done so to prevent the man from suspecting, he did not need to guess at the young woman's identity. In spite of her normally blonde hair having been dyed brunette and fixed in a different style to their last meeting, he had recognized her at first sight. Belle Starr, the lady outlaw, was on very close and intimate terms with his *amigo,* Mark Counter, and the Kid had met her on more than one occasion.[1]

Already alerted by the bellhop's description of "Guillemot" to the possibility of something being wrong, the Kid had been worried about the absence of the "big square-head." Taken with Belle Starr's warning head-shake, the partially open door had offered an answer to that question. Her signal had also been warning that it might be inadvisable for him to shake hands with "Guillemot."

"Without wishing to offend you," the man said, without acknowledging the Kid's suggestion regarding his and Belle's identities, "but you have proof that you are General Hardin's representative."

"Nope," the Kid answered, moving around so that he could keep the left side door under observation; but doing it in a casual and, apparently, accidental manner.

"You haven't?" the man growled.

"I didn't reckon I'd need any," the Kid explained, "seeing's my boss, Cap'n Fog'll be along soon. Him being Ole Devil's nephew 'n' all, he's the one who'll be doing all the talking."

"And where is Captain Fog now?" the man asked, his face showing no emotion.

"Down to Shelby's livery barn," the Kid lied, with such an

1. How Mark Counter's romance with Belle Starr started, progressed and ended is told in: the "The Bounty On Belle Starr's Scalp" episode of *Troubled Range, The Bad Bunch, Rangeland Hercules,* the "The Lady Known As Belle" episode of *The Hard Riders and Guns in the Night.* Two occasions when she met the Ysabel Kid are told in: *Hell in the Palo Duro* and *Go Back to Hell.*

air of sincerity that he might have been telling the truth with his hand on a bible. "We've only just now hit town and he sent me along to let you know he's coming."

"*Ach* so!" the man ejaculated. "And he will be here soon?"

"Why sure."

"I trust that you had an uneventful journey, Mr.—" Belle put in.

"So peaceable I was like to sleep all the way for want of something to do, ma'am," the Kid replied. "Why wouldn't we have?"

"One hears such terrible stories about this wild frontier country," Belle explained, with a wide-eyed awe which was amusing to anybody who knew her true nature. "What with marauding Indians and outlaws lurking behind each and every bush."

"We didn't see a one of either, ma'am," the Kid declared. "Which doesn't surprise *me* none."

"Why ever not?" Belle inquired.

"Without wanting to sound boastful, ma'am." the Kid elaborated, looking at the girl and sensing that the man was paying very keen attention to the conversation, "anybody's knows Cap'n Fog 'n' me, which most folks out here do, wouldn't want to lock horns with us."

"You think so, huh?" barked the man.

"Mister," the Kid replied, turning coldly mocking eyes back to his challenger. "I *know* so for sure. Was a feller once tried to have us gunned down. Hadn't the guts, or was too smart, to try it his-self, so he hired him a couple of *pistolero valientes*—happen you-all know what they are—?"

"I know," the man conceded.

"Well, sir," the Kid went on. "He paid 'em real good money to do it. Only, once they'd got that money, why they just headed over the border and he never saw them—or his money—again."

For all his surreptitious, but keen-eyed, scrutiny, the Kid could not detect any trace of concern on the man's hard face. Yet he sensed that his comments had aroused some emotion.

"Well," the Kid continued, deciding against forcing the issue. "I've done what I was sent for, so I'll be drifting along. There's this lil Mexican *senorita* I know—"

"How long will it be before Captain Fog comes?" "Guillemot" interrupted.

"About an hour or so," the Kid replied. "His Cousin Betty's coming in on the noon stage 'n' he wants to be on hand to meet her."

"Very well," "Guillemot" said, glancing at the partially open door as if trying to make up his mind. Then he shrugged and went on. "Will you go and tell him that I'd be obliged if he could come to see me straight away? We can attend to our business in time for him to meet his cousin."

"I'll do that," the Kid promised. "*Adios*, Mrs. Guillemot, ma'am. It's been right pleasant making your acquaintance."

While speaking, the Kid was crossing the room. He walked in such a manner that at no time was the left side door out of his range of vision. Returning the Winchester to his right hand, but taking the precaution of grasping it in the same way, he nodded to the man and Belle, then left.

After the door had closed, the second man came out of the bedroom. Burly, with close-cropped blond hair, his town suit was of a cheaper quality than "Guillemot's" garments. Scowling, he thrust the short-barrelled Webley Bulldog revolver he was holding beneath his open jacket and into the cross-draw holster on the left side of his waist-belt.

"Shall we wait for Fog?" the man asked and, although he spoke English very well, there was a trace of a hard Germanic accent in his voice.

"You can," Belle Starr replied, before "Guillemot" could speak. "But *I'm* leaving right now. And, if you've any sense, you'll do the same."

"What do you mean?" "Guillemot" demanded.

"When Ram Turtle asked me to come down here with you and lend you a hand, I don't think he knew—and I certainly didn't—that the people you were after was the OD Connected," Belle answered, standing up and lifting free the reticule which was dangling by its draw-strings from the back of her chair. Holding it in her left hand, she slipped the right into its mouth and went on, "That's one outfit I don't intend to lock horns with—"

"We came here to 'lock horns,' as you put it, with the man who has been sent to act as guide for the Ox," "Guillemot" protested. "And you being here was to lull his suspicions."

"That's true," Belle conceded. "And it was a good plan, or

would have been if it had worked. Now I've seen who we're up against, I'm not surprised that Urizza either backed out or failed. If I'd known who was involved, I could have told you that there'd be more than one of them coming and no two-bit *pistolero* like Urizza would stop them."

"The Ox only asked for one man to be sent," "Guillemot" objected.

"Or so you were told," the girl countered. "Have you seen a copy of the letter?"

"No," "Guillemot" admitted. "But my informant knew what was in it."

"Maybe he only *guessed* at what was said," Belle suggested. "He might not have had a chance to read it."

"*He'd* have the chance all right," the burly man put in. "Are we going to wait for Fog to come and catch him like—"

"Like you *didn't* catch the Kid?" Belle corrrected, although the words had not been directed at her.

"You *knew* him?" "Guillemot" growled, eyeing the girl suspiciously.

"I've seen him and all the rest of Ole Devil's floating outfit," Belle replied.

"When Fog comes—" the second man began.

"He'll be ready for trouble," Belle interrupted. "Hasn't it sunk into your head yet that the Kid knew Mr. Ehlring isn't the Ox?"

"How could he know?" the burly man asked worriedly.

"Maybe your informant didn't know as much as you think," Belle answered. "There could have been a description of the Ox in the letter, or perhaps there was supposed to be a password." She looked at Ehlring and continued. "You saw the way he acted. He either guessed, or knew, that Werra was in the bedroom."

"I should have come out—!" Werra barked.

"If you had, there'd have been shooting," Belle assured him. "Which's what we were trying to avoid. I tell you, he *knew* he wasn't meeting the Ox. Now he's gone to tell Dusty Fog. And I don't aim to be here when they arrive."

"There'll only be the two of them," Werra declared truculently. "Let's wait for them and—"

"A mistake like *that* could get you shot," Belle warned.

"You'll be up against the fastest gun in Texas and the Kid's nearly as good. There'll be no way you can take them by surprise, or catch them without shooting. Even *if* you survived, the Ox would hear about it when he gets here and the letter of introduction from General Hardin wouldn't do us any good."

"So what do we do?" Ehlring wanted to know, gritting out the words angrily.

"Get out of here," Belle answered, backing towards the door with her right hand still concealed in the reticule. "And out of San Antonio."

"We came here to do a—!" Ehlring commenced.

"Then you can stay on and try to do it," Belle told him, halting at the door. "But I'm going somewhere that's a whole heap safer than this town's going to be."

"Damn it—!" Ehlring snarled, taking a step forward in a menacing fashion.

"You're not going to *try* to stop me, are you?" Belle challenged, showing neither alarm nor fear although her right hand came nearer to the top of the reticule and was clearly grasping something. "I wouldn't advise *that*."

"All right," Ehlring grunted, after having studied the girl's coldly determined face and attitude for a few seconds. "Go if you want."

"I thought you'd see it my way," Belle declared. Then she tightened the draw strings so that the reticule would remain on her right hand until she used the left to reach behind and open the door. "There's *no* way you can make your idea work and, if you've any sense, you'll get out of town as quickly as possible. That's what I intend to do."

"You think its *that* serious?" Ehlring inquired, impressed despite his aversion to receiving even sound advice from a woman.

"I *know* it is," Belle assured him. "Which's why I'm pulling out. *Adios,* gentlemen. If you don't think I've earned my pay, see Ram Turtle and tell him I said to let you have half of it back."

With that, the girl stepped into the passage and closed the door. Looking each way, to satisfy herself that she was unobserved, she released the Remington Double Derringer with which she had ensured her safe departure and brought her hand from the reticule. Going to the main staircase, she gazed down at the reception lobby. However, although she saw nothing to alarm her, she glanced at the door of the suite and turned to go up to the second floor.

"She's right," Ehlring admitted to his companion, after Belle had left. "Let's get out of here."

"Shall I go and see the desk clerk?" Werra inquired, as they crossed the room.[2]

"No," Ehlring replied. "There's no need. We can't get a man with the Ox now. He'll have to go through Eagle Pass, so we'll wait there and follow him when he arrives."

2. If the plan had worked, Werra was to have interviewed the desk clerk and told him that, having learned of a plot to rob Guillemot, he and his partner had taken steps to prevent it. So his partner had pretended to be the victim and had acted as bait. To avoid the kind of publicity which would have been detrimental to the hotel's reputation, they had already dealt with and would remove the would-be-robber. However, if Guillemot was to learn of the attempt, he would leave immediately, losing the hotel a valuable and influential guest. The only way this could be avoided was for the clerk to ensure that no mention of the "Pinkerton agents'" activities was made when Guillemot arrived. From what they had seen of the clerk, they had felt sure that he would do as they wished. Then they would have sent a man, hired by Belle Starr and supplied with whatever means of identification the Kid had been carrying, to pose as Ole Devil Hardin's representative.

CHAPTER EIGHT

I'm *Very* Fast With A Gun

"Good afternoon," Belle Boyd greeted, as a tall, handsome and well-dressed young man opened the door of the Sandford Hotel's Room 21. "I'm Betty Hardin and I've come to see Mr. Guillemot."

"Show the lady in, Silk," called a booming voice.

"He's with me," Belle explained in an off-hand manner, as the man looked pointedly at the Ysabel Kid. She contrived to sound as if she regarded her companion as being of no importance. "He can wait out here if you wish."

"Aw, Miss Hardin," the Kid protested. "You know your grandpappy said I should stick with you—"

"All right, Silk," the booming voice went on. "Show them both in."

Moving aside, the young man allowed Belle and the Kid to walk by. Then he closed the door and followed them. They ignored him for the moment, being more interested in the room's second occupant.

There was something almost bovine about Octavius Xavier Guillemot which might have accounted for his nickname, even without the coincidence of his initials. It was not the sleek, awesome majesty of a longhorn bull, but more of the massive yet placcid solidity of a draught oxen. Six foot in height, he was built on an enormous scale. His face was bland, with bulbous pink cheeks, lips and chins set on a thick neck. The eyes, made to look small by the rolls of fat around them, were dark but alert and his curly brown hair was tinged with grey yet still luxurious. Obviously his excellently cut black town suit had been tailored to his measure, for it covered his ample body perfectly without lessening the bulk underneath.

While studying Guillemot, Belle and the Kid were conscious that he was subjecting them to equally careful scrutiny. The girl was dressed as she had been during her meeting with the Kid, except that she no longer wore a wig. For his part, the Kid had left his rifle behind at Ma Laughlin's rooming house.

Finding Belle Starr with the two imposters had presented the Kid with a dilemma in how he should deal with them. While his first instinct had been to find some way to capture and question the men, he had seen a major objection to such an action. It was unlikely that he could bring it off single-handed without gun play. Yet to call on Town Marshal Anse Dale for assistance would have meant involving the lady out-law. The Kid had been disinclined to do that. Not only had she given him a warning which had steered him out of a trap, she had been of the greatest assistance to Dusty Fog and himself in the town of Hell.

With that thought in mind, the Kid had waited in conceal-ment and followed the two men when they had left by the rear entrance. They had gone to a smaller hotel. Reappearing in a few minutes carrying carpetbags, they had gone to a livery barn and collected a rig. Although the Kid had not followed them, he had felt sure that they were leaving San Antonio and would not be coming back.

Discussing the matter with Belle Boyd, while they were on their way to meet Guillemot, the Kid had found that she ap-proved of his decision. They would, she had said, be able to turn his failure to do anything about the men to their advantage.

On arriving at the hotel, Belle and the Kid had been informed by a clearly perturbed clerk that Mr. Guillemot had arrived. Although it had been apparent that he would have liked to say more, he had made no reference to the Kid's previous visit. Instead, he had ordered the same bellhop to take them upstairs. The youngster had been just as obviously bubbling with curiosity, but had restrained it.

Passing the visitors, the young man halted slightly to the rear of Guillemot's chair. Dark haired, swarthily handsome, he moved with a swift economy of motion which implied that he would be capable of even greater speed. His brown town suit was expensive and well tailored. Its jacket almost, but not quite, concealed a slight bulge under the left arm-pit. Studying the man, the Kid gave the bulge more attention than the Smith & Wesson American Model of 1869 revolver which was riding in the low-tied fast-draw holster of his Western style gunbelt.

"Miss Hardin?" Guillemot said, advancing around the table and offering a huge right hand.

"I am, sir," Belle lied, noting the way the greeting had been expressed and wondering if the deception would fail.

"I hope you'll pardon me," Guillemot went on, after shaking hands. "But I wonder if you would object to showing me proof of your identity."

"I beg your pardon, *sir?*" Belle snapped, displaying haughty indignation.

"I assure you that I mean no distrust, nor disrespect, my dear young lady," the Ox stated blandly. "But I have good cause for displaying caution."

"I should hope so, indeed!" Belle snorted, then waited with the air of expecting an explanation.

"I discovered, on arriving, that an impostor had come—" Guillemot commenced.

"Hey!" yelped the Kid, with well-simulated alarm. "You mean that feller wasn't working for you?"

"Which fellow?" Belle demanded, turning on the Texan.

"I come 'round earlier, to see if this gent was here—" the Kid began, adopting a sullen and resentful tone.

"Why?" Belle interrupted. "You knew that I would be arriving—"

"What happened, young man?" Guillemot put in, then

swung his gaze to Belle who was registering disapproval. "My pardon for interrupting, Miss Hardin, but you will appreciate my eagerness to learn more about this matter."

"I suppose so," Belle conceded stiffly and, with the air of granting a favor, went on, "Very well, Ysabel, tell Mr. Guillemot all about it."

Watching the by-play the Kid found himself most impressed by the way in which Belle was acting the part she had selected as suitable for their needs. Every word and gesture was that of a rich, arrogant, spoiled and snobbish young woman who was filled with an over-inflated sense of her own importance. He also found amusement in contemplating how Betty Hardin was going to react on hearing about the type of person—one who was completely the opposite to her true nature, in fact— that the Rebel Spy was making her out to be.

However, the Kid was less amused by the way in which the younger of the men was looking at him. There was more than a hint of contempt and mockery on the swarthily handsome face, the emotions clearly having been brought about by seeing the Texan treated in such a fashion by a woman.

"Like I said," the Kid explained and the younger man's thinly veiled disdain did much to help him attain the right kind of attitude. His voice and general bearing conveyed—to the two men at least—an impression of his annoyance over the manner in which the girl had addressed him. "I come 'round here to see if you'd showed up, Mr. Guillemot—"

"Why?" Belle demanded indignantly. "You knew that I was coming."

"Your telegraph message hadn't got to me," the Kid answered sullenly, then returned his gaze to the Ox. "Anyways, I come and asked for you. Got showed up and this feller was in here. He allowed he worked for you and's you'd just gone for a walk. Asked who I was and if I'd gotten anything to prove's I'd been sent by Ole Dev—General Hardin—" The alteration in the name had been made in response to Belle's frown and, having made it, he went on, "When I said I hadn't—"

"Why hadn't you?" the younger man put in.

"He wasn't supposed to come here at all," Belle answered,

glaring angrily at the Kid. "And the letters wouldn't have been of any use to him. They were to introduce my cousin, Captain Dustine Edward Marsden Fog."

"Why isn't Captain Fog here?" Guillemot inquired.

"He was ambushed on the trail and injured," Belle replied, glancing poitedly at the chairs around the table.

"My dear Miss Hardin, how remiss of me!" Guillemot ejaculated, having noticed and interpreted the look correctly. "Please have a seat. You must be tired after your journey."

"A five mile ride is nothing," Belle sniffed, allowing herself to be seated on the chair which the Ox drew out for her. Resting her parasol against it, she dropped her reticule on to her lap.

"*Five* miles—?" the younger man began.

"I was visiting out at the Schofield ranch, *sir,*" Belle told him, showing her disapproval at the interruption and then scowled at the Kid. "You were supposed to come and fetch me. The first thing I knew was when the General's telegraph message arrived."

"I was aiming to—" the Kid commenced, although his attitude suggested that he had had no such intention.

"Tell me about the ambush, *Mr.* Ysabel," Guillemot requested.

"There's not a heap to tell," the Kid declared, but obliged with a description of the affair.

"It could have been somebody with an old score to settle," Guillemot suggested, having resumed his seat.

"Why sure," the Kid agreed. "And that's all I figured it to be, until I got jumped last night here in San Antonio."

"Who by?" Guillemot demanded.

"A feller dressed's a woman was all I saw for sure, and him not plain," the Kid replied. "Was another one, 'cording to the deputy's happened by and chased 'em off. Big and heavy built jasper."

"Could he have been the man who was here?" Guillemot wanted to know.

"Not 'less the deputy called it wrong. The jasper here was tall, but not hefty. Looked like he'd been in the Army. Real bow-necked officer, I'd say."

"They could have been trying to rob you," Guillemot remarked, after darting a questioning look at his companion and receiving a negative shake of the head.

"I'd've thought that, 'cepting they left my money in my pocket," the Kid countered. "Which's one of the reasons I wasn't carrying Ole—the General's letters this morning when I come around."

"Here they are, Mr. Guillemot," Belle said, opening her reticule and extracting three envelopes without allowing its other contents—particularly her Remington Double Derringer—to be seen. "These are the General's letters introducing Cousin Dusty to you along with a copy of the letter which he received from Resin Bowie the Second, a letter of introduction to *Senor* Serrano and the telegraph message telling me to take Cousin Dusty's place. How soon do you wish to start?"

"*You* want to go with *us?*" the younger man put in.

Instead of answering, Belle slowly ran her gaze over the speaker. Then she turned an interrogatory glance at the Ox.

"May I present Mr. Anthony Silk, Miss Hardin?" Guillemot inquired, lifting his gaze from the first of the letters. "He is my secretary, companion and strong right arm."

If the cold scrutiny which the girl returned to Silk meant anything, she felt that the introduction was hardly worth acknowledging as the person in question was of little or no consequence. However, she nodded briefly before finally deigning to reply, "No, *Mr.* Silk. I don't *want* to go with *you.* I intend to take your *employer* to visit *Senor* Serrano, as Resin Bowie the Second requested. You *may* be coming along."

"Shucks, Miss Hardin," the Kid put in, deriving some satisfaction in watching a red flush creeping into Silk's cheeks and anger showing on his face. "I can handle it easy enough. There's no call for you to come along."

"Mr. Bowie asked for the General to send his *personal* representative," Belle reminded the young Texan in her most haughty and overbearing manner. "That means one of his kin, not just a hired hand. All we need from you is that you guide us there and back."

"Ah! So you are to be our guide, young man," Guillemot boomed, watching in a speculative fashion as the Kid's Indian-dark features registered resentment over the girls's words. "Do you know how to find *Casa Serrano?*"

"It's easy enough done," the Kid replied, noticing that Silk was showing pleasure at the way Belle had spoken to him. "We'll cross the Rio Grande up Eagle Pass way, then head south until we hit the *Rio de la Babia*. From there, we'll go up the *Rio Ventoso*. *Casa Serrano's* maybe fifty miles along it."

"There doesn't seem to be any great difficulty in finding it," Silk remarked, addressing the Ox.

"Well now," the Kid drawled. "I'd say that depends on who-all's going."

"I intended only a small party," Guillemot answered, as once again the words had clearly been directed at him. "Just myself, Silk and General Hardin's representative. But in view of what has happened—"

"I can assure you that Ysabel is a very competent guide," Belle declared, deliberately misinterpreting the cause of the Ox's and Silk's eyes swinging towards her.

"I don't doubt *that*—" Guillemot began.

"And if you're concerned on my behalf, don't be," Belle advised. "I've been handling and riding horses practically all my life." Her gaze flickered at the younger man in an insultingly challenging way and she continued, "It won't be *me* who you have to worry about slowing us down."

"That's for sure," the Kid confirmed, before he could stop himself. "Only it's not being slowed down's'll be all we have to worry about."

"Why?" Guillemot asked. "Is the terrain difficult?"

"Nope," the Kid replied. "Fact being, most of the way it'll be real easy going."

"Then what—"

"Mexican *bandidos*, Mr. Guillemot. Could even be some Yaqui Injuns. We're likely to run into 'em between the Rio Grande and *Casa Serrano*, even if that jasper who was in here when I first came doesn't figure on cutting in again."

"I don't follow you," Guillemot stated, although his attitude suggested that he had an idea of what the Texan was driving at.

"He was here after *something*—" the Kid began, having decided that—with his "resentment" over "Betty Hardin's" treatment made noticeable—he should let the Ox see that he had qualities which might be useful.

"Just what does that mean?" Silk demanded, drawing a disapproving frown from the older man.

"Just what it says, mister," the Kid answered, matching the other's thinly concealed hostility. A glance at Belle told him that she felt he was doing the right thing. "He wasn't in here, letting on's how he worked for Mr. Guillemot, just so's he could get out of the sun."

"Possibly he was a thief and said what he did when you surprised him," the Ox suggested blandly.

"If that's all he was, he sure's hell knowed some mighty smart questions 'n' answers," the Kid responded sardonically. "Anyways, Marshal Dale's a pretty slick lawman. Is that what he reckons the feller was?"

"We haven't reported the matter to the marshal," Guillemot confessed.

"Why not?" the Kid wanted to know. "If I'd got word that somebody'd been in my room and letting folks think's he worked for me when he didn't, I'd sure's shooting want him found."

"I'd prefer not to have anything which might draw attention to me," Guillemot explained. "After all, I hadn't even arrived. So there was nothing here for him to steal—"

"There could've been, happen I'd've been toting along those letters from General Hardin," the Kid pointed out. "Happen that feller'd've jumped me then took them 'n' my body out of here, you could be talking to one of his *amigos* right now."

"We might be," Silk remarked.

"Happen you think so, go send for the marshal to tell you who I am," the Kid offered. "I won't stop you."

"I don't think we need do *that*," Guillemot stated, waving a fat hand at the letters. "These are satisfactory evidence of your *bona fides*." Then he eyed the Kid with a greater interest which its recipient and Belle found satisfying. "And *you* certainly don't strike me as being a *man* who it would be easy to 'jump' as you put it. What do you think, Miss Hardin?"

"I wouldn't care to be the man who tried it," Belle said and, for almost the first time in the conversation, was completely sincere. "But I must also agree with Ysabel. You should have told the marshal. The desk clerk or the manager is sure to—"

"That isn't likely," Guillemot contradicted politely. "I have left them in no doubts as to my feelings on the matter. And for a good reason. The impostor may have been here, as Mr. Ysabel so shrewdly deduced, to replace General Hardin's representative with a man of his own. Which implies that others know of what we hope to achieve."

"Then surely you should tell Marshal Dale," Belle suggested.

"I think *not*, Miss Hardin," Guillemot stated and there was hardness under his bland tones, giving the girl and the Kid their first insight to his true nature. "Once he started his inquiries, they would attract attention and could cause still other people to suspect that my visit might be for more than just a hunting trip. *That* could only increase our difficulties."

"You mean that somebody else'd figure on getting ole Jim Bowie's knife from you," the Kid put in.

"If they knew we had it," Guillemot agreed. "We are dealing with something of considerable historical value. Such things command high prices."

"And folks're likely to try *real* hard to get 'em," the Kid went on. "Fact being, they've already started at it."

"So it seems," Guillemot conceded.

"So it *is*" the Kid corrected. "Maybe more'n one bunch of 'em. The *hombre* who got away after the bushwhack wasn't the same's I met here, nor with them's jumped me on the street—"

"Go on," Guillemot prompted.

"That being so," the Kid obliged. "I reckon we should telegraph the General and have him send the rest of the floating outfit along."

"We don't need them," Silk commented.

"Comes trouble and we will," the Kid answered. "Because, even if all these yahoos aren't in cahoots, there's more of 'em than I can handle on my lonesome."

"I'll be with you," Silk pointed out.

"*You?*" the Kid sniffed, wanting to see what kind of a reaction he could evoke.

"I'm *very* fast with a gun," Silk announced, showing anger. "Perhaps you think differently?"

"I wouldn't know," the Kid answered. "Never having seen you use one."

"Perhaps you'd like to see me now?" Silk suggested icily, lifting his right hand as if to let it hover over the butt of the Smith & Wesson, but held horizontally. His left rose slowly, as if in a nervous gesture, to stroke at the lapel of his jacket.

Taking in his challenger's appearance, the Kid drew rapid conclusions. He had grown up around gun fighters and had met many of the best. So he could differentiate between the real thing and a show-off. Unless he was much mistaken, dude or not, Silk came into the former classification. There was the indefinable aura about him of a man who was capable of killing without hesitation.

"Well now," the Kid drawled at the completion of his summation, sounding so mild that Belle—if not the two men—realized he was at a state of complete readiness for action. "Happen you're so all-fired fast, I don't reckon's I would at that." Then, as he saw the mocking twist which came to Silk's lips, he hooked his thumbs into his gunbelt and went on, "Only I never took to looking like I've backed down, neither."

Even if Belle had not duplicated her companion's estimation of Silk's potential, she would have sensed it. So she glanced at Guillemot, who was sitting with both hands resting before him on the table. She could read nothing on the bland, pink face and wondered if she should intervene immediately or wait to see what he would do.

The decision was taken from Belle's hands by a knocking on the door.

"Will you see who that is, Silk?" Guillemot requested, still without giving any evidence of his feelings.

For a moment, the younger man neither moved nor spoke. Belle, for one, could sense that he wanted to force a showdown.

Then, making an almost visible effort, Silk relaxed and walked with short, angry steps across the room to open the door.

"Good afternoon," said a feminine voice from the passage, "Mr. Turtle of Fort Worth asked me to drop by and say 'hello' to Mr. Guillemot for him."

Belle and the Kid exchanged glances!

Instantly, in a casual-seeming manner, the girl lowered her hands to the reticule on her lap.

Although the Kid had not done so while confronting Silk, he let his right hand drop and turned it palm outwards alongside the worn walnut grips of his old Dragoon Colt.

Even without being able to see the speaker, they both knew that she was Belle Starr.

CHAPTER NINE

The Son-Of-A-Bitch *Is Fast*

"Ask the young lady to come in, Silk," Octavius Xavier Guillemot requested, as the swarthily handsome young man looked at him for guidance.

Once again, after briefly studying their host, Belle Boyd and the Ysabel Kid exchanged swift glances. Neither of them knew what to make of this latest and most unexpected development. However, they had failed to detect any suggestion that the fat man had discerned something of their perturbation and had given the order so as to try them out. So each was seeking assurance that the other appreciated the situation and was prepared to meet any eventuality. Having satisfied themselves on that point, they turned their attention towards the door.

There was, Belle and the Kid realized, a considerable threat to the success of their deception. While they were now sufficiently forewarned to be able to conceal the fact that they recognized Belle Starr, the same did not apply with her. Finding herself suddenly confronted by them and being aware of the

Rebel Spy's true identity,[1] she might inadvertently say or do something to betray them.

Or, in view of how the lady outlaw had announced herself, the betrayal might be deliberate. Her reference to "Mr. Turtle of Fort Worth" had been as significant to Belle Boyd and the Kid[2] as it had appeared to be to the Ox. Ram Turtle was a man of considerable importance to the criminal element of Texas, owning a saloon on the outskirts of that city at which wanted men could find shelter or leave messages. According to Belle Starr, she had been sent by Turtle to make contact with Guillemot.

All of which raised two vitally important points for Belle Boyd and the Kid.

Why had the Ox asked the lady outlaw to come in, guessing what she must be, while they were present?

Could he suspect them and **hop**ed that Ram Turtle's agent would be able to confirm or **deny** their identities?

Thinking fast, before Silk could carry out his instructions, Belle Boyd started to stand up, raised her voice and said, "If it isn't convenient for Ysabel and I to stay, Mr. Guillemot—"

By doing so, the Rebel Spy had two things in mind. She hoped to give a warning to the lady outlaw, in case Belle Starr might have no desire to expose them. Or to be in a better position to protect herself if the need should arise.

"It isn't, Miss Hardin," the Ox boomed in tones loud enough to accidentally, or deliberately, give the girl who was entering further information.

Belle Starr had changed her clothes since the Kid had last seen her and, from all appearances, had been doing some travelling. She had on a black Stetson, a tight-rolled scarlet bandana knotted around her throat, a fringed buckskin jacket over an open-necked grey shirt and a doeskin divided skirt from beneath which emerged brown riding boots. All the garments were spattered with a coating of dust. The reticule had gone, being replaced by a leather quirt which was dangling by its carrying strap from her left wrist.

"I'm sorry, Mr. Guillemot," the lady outlaw said, coming

---

1. How Belle Boyd and Belle Starr first met is told in: *The Bad Bunch*.
2. How the Ysabel Kid came into contact with Ram Turtle is told in: *Set Texas Back on her Feet*.

to a halt and looking at the two men and the girl around the table. "If I'd realized that you had visitors, I wouldn't have come."

Watching the other young woman, Belle Boyd was impressed by her self control. Either she had recognized the Rebel Spy's voice and understood the warning it was giving, or she was exceptionally good at concealing her emotions. No matter which it might be, she gave no hint of knowing Belle Boyd or the Kid.

Nor of betraying them.

"I'm pleased you did, Miss—" Guillemot answered, coming to his feet and advancing with his right hand extended.

"Beauregard," Starr replied, shaking hands. "Magnolia Beauregard."

"This is a pleasure, Miss Beauregard," Guillemot stated, then indicated his other guests. "Perhaps you know Miss Betty Hardin and Mr. Ysabel?"

"We haven't met," Starr lied, but without any evidence of it showing in her voice or actions. "But of course everybody has heard of the Ysabel Kid. It's a pleasure to make your acquaintance, sir. And yours, Miss Hardin."

"I hope that you haven't heard of Mr. Ysabel in your official capacity, Miss Beauregard?" Guillemot inquired, then swung his gaze to the Kid. "Just a little joke, sir, with no offence meant or, I hope, taken. You wouldn't think it to look at her, but Miss Beauregard is a detective from the Pinkerton Agency."

"Wee dogie!" the Kid ejaculated, guessing that Starr was as surprised as himself to learn of her employment. "I ain't never yet met a real-live lady detective before."

"A *lady* detective," Boyd went on, having duplicated the Kid's summation. It ruled out the possibility that Starr had attempted to pass herself off in such a capacity as a means of pulling a confidence trick or robbery with the Ox as its victim. Wanting to give Starr a clue to the part she was playing, her voice expressed thinly-veiled disdain and snobbish disapproval. "My! Whatever next."

"A girl has to earn her livings as best she can, Miss Hardin," Starr answered in chilly tones. "Or *some* of us do."

"I suppose so," Boyd sniffed, then turned away from the other girl. "If you have things to discuss with this—*lady*—Mr.

Guillemot, I can come back later."

"There's no need for that, as our business also concerns you," the Ox replied. "Please be seated. And you, Miss Beauregard."

"Very well, if you're sure that we're not intruding," Boyd consented, although her attitude displayed that she did not care for the idea of sharing the same table as the "lady detective."

While the Kid was satisfied that the danger of being exposed had passed, at least for the time being, he did not relax in his vigilance where Guillemot's secretary was concerned. Anthony Silk had closed the door and crossed the room to take up his position behind his employer's chair. Although he darted a challenging glare at the young Texan, he did not attempt to resume the situation which had been developing before Belle Starr's arrival. Sensing that any furtherance of it might need to be pushed to the limit, the Kid was willing to let things ride. Something warned him, however, that he and the secretary might have to lock horns in the future. Nor did he sell Silk short. Dude or not, there was a *very* dangerous man.

"I suppose you are wondering why I have hired a member of the Pinkerton Agency, Miss Hardin, Mr. Ysabel?" Guillemot remarked, after the girls had taken their seats and he was settled on his chair.

"I am," Boyd agreed, wondering what excuse would be made.

"Wouldn't be to keep a look out for folks's might have a hankering to lay hands on old Jim Bowie's knife, would it?" the Kid inquired, wanting to carry on with the process of impressing the Ox.

"It would, sir," Guillemot admitted and his expression suggested that the process was producing the required result. "I don't know to whom, but I have reason to believe that a rumor of what I hope to do—for the Bowie family—has been circulated."

"You mean somebody's been talking out of turn, huh?" asked the Kid, having noticed that the reference to the Bowie family appeared to have been an afterthought.

"It would appear so," Guillemot confirmed.

"Perhaps your *lady* detective could find out who did it,"

Boyd suggested and received a frown from Starr that was surprisingly genuine.

"There's no need for her to waste time on *that*," Guillemot declared, just a shade too quickly Boyd thought. "Silk has already found out that my valet was responsible."

"Where's this here 'valley' at now?" the Kid inquired, deciding against casting doubt on the secretary's judgement.

"I discharged him without a reference, naturally," Guillemot answered, but there was something in his bland tones which implied that the subject was closed as far as further discussion was concerned. "He refused to say to whom he had sold the information, unfortunately. That was why I consulted the Pinkerton Agency."

"Have you found out who it is, Miss——?" Boyd inquired, her attitude suggesting that a "lady detective's" social standing was not sufficient to warrant remembering her name.

"Beauregard," Starr supplied icily, guessing what kind of a character the Rebel Spy was portraying and sharing the Kid's view on the excellence of the performance. "And my findings are confidential, *Miss Hardin*."

"Come come, Miss Beauregard," Guillemot boomed jovially. "You can speak freely. Miss Hardin, Mr. Ysabel and Silk are all in my confidence."

"Well, if that's how you want it, all right," Starr replied, sounding as if she disapproved but felt she was absolved of all blame if things should go wrong. "As far as I can make out, there are two separate groups involved, one French and one German. In fact, the Germans were in this room this morning."

"We know all about that," Boyd declared haughtily, having noticed an exchange of glances between the Ox and his secretary. "I suppose you learned in the same way we did, from the desk clerk?"

"Not exactly," Starr answered. "I'd come to see if you'd arrived, Mr. Guillemot, and was told that you had. So I came up and was just in time to see Ehlring and Werra leaving the suite."

"Why didn't you stop them?" Boyd demanded, feeling such a comment would be expected from her.

"I didn't know that Mr. Guillemot wasn't here and they

weren't behaving suspiciously," Starr told her. "For all I knew, they could have been paying him a visit. Of course, as soon as I'd knocked and didn't get an answer, I went downstairs. The clerk told me that 'Mr. Guillemot' had just left, so I went to look for them. They were driving away in a rig, so I got my horse and followed."

"Why didn't you fetch the marshal and have them arrested?" Boyd wanted to know.

"Because Mr. Guillemot had said that he didn't want any attention drawn to him," Starr countered. "And the way I see it, if there's any complaint about how I've handled things, it should come from my employer."

"Well *really*—!" Boyd squealed indignantly, starting to rise.

"Ladies, *please,*" Guillemot put in soothingly. "Although I don't condone how she answered you, Miss Hardin, I am satisfied that Miss Beauregard acted for the best."

"Very well," Boyd sniffed, sitting down.

"Where did they go to, Miss Beauregard?" the Ox inquired, with peace restored.

"Out of town, on the south-bound trail," Starr replied. "I followed them for as long as I dared and they weren't showing any sign of turning back."

"Do you-all reckon they will be, ma'am?" asked the Kid.

"They *might,* but they didn't look like they meant to as they'd got baggage in the rig," Starr answered. "They'd know that Mr. Guillemot would hear about what they'd been up to when he arrived and might figure that the town marshal'd be set to looking for them. So they could just keep on going."

"You say there were *two* of them, Miss Beauregard?" Guillemot asked and glanced quizzically at the Kid.

"I only *saw* one of them," the young Texan admitted, in response to the unasked question. "Which the other could've been in one of the other rooms. Fact being, the door to that 'n'—" he pointed a finger to the left, "was open a mite. So that's where he likely was hidden."

"*Two* of them," Silk put in, "and they let you walk out."

"Why not?" countered the Kid. "I wasn't carrying the letters's they was after—but I did have my ole 'yellow boy.'"

"Your what?" Guillemot asked, throwing a cold scowl at his secretary as he spoke.

"Winchester," the Kid explained. "Folks call it that 'cause of its brass frame. Anyways, I reckon that, seeing's I didn't have what they wanted, they figured it wasn't worth chancing making a fuss."

"That's true enough," Guillemot said firmly and, clearly wanting to change the subject, he looked at the lady outlaw. "So you don't think they'll be coming back, Miss Beauregard?"

"I'd be surprised if they do," Starr answered. "Especially if they think you've told Marshal Dale. He's a well-deserved name for being an efficient lawman."

"Then we'll hope that we've seen the last of them," Guillemot declared.

"We may have seen the last of *them*," Starr conceded. "But not of the other two."

"Which other two?" the Ox barked.

"The Frenchmen," Starr replied.

"Haven't *they* left town?" Boyd asked.

"Not unless they went since I came up here," Starr assured her.

"What do you mean?" Guillemot demanded.

"They're in the Bon Ton Restaurant across the street," Starr explained. "Seated by a window, so they can watch the front entrance of the hotel."

For a moment, none of the others spoke. The Kid looked at Belle Boyd, then turned his gaze towards the two men. Nothing showed on Guillemot's face. However, Silk seemed pensive and his left hand was once more rising to stroke at the lapel of his jacket.

"Are you sure that they're watching us?" Guillemot finally asked.

"I am," Starr confirmed. "They call one of them 'Slippers,' he's a swish—"

"A 'swish?'" the Ox repeated, sounding puzzled.

"It means he likes men, not girls," Starr interpreted. "If Miss Hardin doesn't mind me saying so."

"Does he dress up like a woman, too?" Boyd inquired, before she could stop herself. Then she contrived to look coy, although apparently pretending to act broadminded. "I've heard people like that sometimes do."

"I've never *seen* him doing it," Starr confessed, wondering what had prompted such a question. "The other one's name is Vernet. He seems to have broken his arm, at least he's wearing it in a sling."

On the point of speaking, the Kid caught a quickly delivered warning shake from Belle Boyd's head. For a moment, he was puzzled. Then he realized what the prohibitive signal had meant. As he had told the other two men that he had been knocked unconscious by his attackers the previous night, he should not have known about Vernet's injury.

"One of the feller's jumped me just after I hit town was dressed like a woman," the young Texan drawled, revising his comment. "That'd be the sort of thing a swish'd do happen he was wanting a disguise. Anyways, I don't reckon it'll do any harm happen I drift over 'n' take a look at 'em."

"Would you recognize them?" Guillemot inquired.

"Likely not," the Kid admitted. "But they just might think I had 'n' do something to give 'em away. I figure it's worth taking a look."

"So do I," Silk remarked. "If they are after us, it will be worth knowing."

"There's more to it than that," the Kid pointed out. "Happen they did jump me, we can get 'em off our trail."

"How?" Guillemot asked.

"Easy enough," the Kid replied. "The marshal'll toss 'em in the pokey."

"And keep *you* here as a witness," Guillemot protested.

"He won't if *I* ask him not to—in the General's name," Boyd put in.

"What do you intend to do, Mr. Ysabel?" Guillemot inquired.

"Just go on over, like I was fixing to have a meal, and look 'em over," the Kid explained. "Then, happen I reckon it was them, I'll pass word for the marshal. Like Miss Hardin says, he'll do a favor for General Hardin and'll hold 'em. Then he can turn 'em loose tomorrow after we've pulled out."

"It's possible that they know our destination," Guillemot warned. "If so, they could follow us."

"Let 'em," the Kid stated. "They might be real he-coons where they come from, but I figure I can hand them their needings once they get out on the range. That's *my* kind of country."

"It's certainly worth trying," Guillemot admitted.

"I'd better come with you, Ysabel," Boyd remarked, rising as the Kid turned to leave. "Cowhands don't usually eat at the Bon Ton."

"Perhaps you and I had better go, too, Miss Beauregard," Silk suggested.

"Sure," Starr agreed, dusting off her clothes. "I could use a meal. How about you, Mr. Guillemot?"

"I think not, young lady," Ox replied. "They could become suspicious if we all arrive."

Although the Kid did not agree with the comment, he kept his thoughts to himself. Leaving the suite with the two girls and Silk, he suggested that they should try to avoid being seen crossing the street. To do so would either scare off the men, or at least allow preparations to be made for their arrival. It was Belle Starr who proposed that they went out by the rear entrance and kept the neighboring buildings between them until they were beyond the pair's range of vision, entering the Bon Ton Restaurant by its side door instead of from the front.

There was little conversation as the party left the building in the way that the lady outlaw had suggested. The Kid was wondering why Silk, who had shown some animosity towards him, had offered to accompany them. However, he put the matter from his thoughts as they approached the side door and entered the Bon Ton Restaurant.

The dining room was, the Kid noted with mixed feelings, almost empty. While that reduced their chances of remaining unnoticed by the men they were seeking, it lessened the danger of harmless bystanders being hurt in the event of gun play. Only a few people and a single waitress were present, none of them near to the pair who were of such interest to the Kid's party.

The two men were still sitting at the table by the window. Both were well-dressed, the shorter of them almost fussily so. As the two Belles, the Kid and Silk came through the door, the taller and more bulky of the pair glanced in their direction. Stiffening noticeably, he spoke in a low tone to his companion.

Then both of them gazed briefly at the front of the hotel. It was obvious that they found the quartet's arrival disconcerting. What was more, from the way they were acting, the Kid decided that—despite his change of clothing and being much cleaner than on the previous night—they recognized him as their would-be victim.

"They know you, L—Kid," Starr said quietly, changing the name just in time as she remembered that there had been no mention of the young Texan's full name.

Darting a look at Silk, Belle Boyd concluded that he had not noticed the lady outlaw's near error. Having removed his hat, he was hanging it on the rack by the door. Then he turned his gaze to the Kid, who was placing his Stetson alongside it.

"Let's go over," Silk suggested, although the words came out more as a command. "Keep well behind us, ladies. There could be trouble."

Without waiting for the Kid to say whether he approved or not, Silk started to walk across the room. Following, the young Texan moved until he was at his companion's left side and about a yard away. While he approved in general of the other's instructions—if not of the manner in which they had been given—he could see one basic flaw in them. Under normal conditions, neither of the girls would have needed to be relegated to a position of safety. Each of them was fully capable of taking care of herself and knew better than to get in the way if there should be any shooting. He accepted that such standards would not be applicable in the case of "Betty Hardin," as the Rebel Spy was portraying her. So she and, probably, the "lady Pinkerton agent" would be better kept out of the possible line of fire.

Against that, the sight of the Kid and Silk approaching, while the girls fell behind, was almost certain to confirm any suspicions the two men might be experiencing over the possibility of their having been identified as his assailants.

Watching Slippers and Vernet, the Kid concluded that his summation on the latter point was correct. As he and Silk continued to draw nearer, with the girls falling even further to the rear and moving aside, the pair started to display agitation.

Glancing at Silk, the Kid found that he was once again stroking the lapel.

No, not *stroking!*

He was *grasping* it!

Something told the Kid that his earlier thoughts had been correct. Silk's action was not merely a nervous gesture.

Slowly, the two men at the table eased back their chairs. They stood up in such a way that they confronted the Kid and Silk. Vernet's right arm was in a sling, but his left hand was reaching underneath it and the side of his jacket. Acting in just as apparently a casual fashion, Slippers raised his right forearm towards the horizontal and its elbow pressed against his ribs. Instantly, a Remington Double Derringer attached to the end of a metal rod was propelled into his palm.

"Look out!" Silk shouted and his left hand drew open the lapel.

From the corner of his eye, even as he responded to the danger, the Kid saw his companion's right hand whip across and under the jacket. It had barely disappeared when it gave a rapid forward twisting motion and emerged holding a short-barrelled revolver.

Although the Kid's right hand had already turned palm out-wards and enfolded the Dragoon's butt, making the movement without the need for conscious guidance, he still had not cleared leather when Silk's weapon crashed.

"The son-of-a-bitch *is* fast!" was the thought which passed fleetingly through the Kid's mind.

It came and went in a flash, for there were other and far more important matters to occupy the young Texan's attention.

Silk was undoubtedly fast and certainly deadly, as the Kid had suspected he might be during the confrontation in Guillemot's suite. However, he appeared to possess a very poor tactical sense.

With the Remington Double Derringer already in his hand and pointing towards the Kid, Slippers was far more dangerous than his companion. Clearly hampered by his injury, Vernet had not even brought out the revolver which he was attempting to draw when Silk's bullet struck him between the eyes and slammed him lifeless against the wall.

Only two things saved the Kid. The lightning speed of his Comanche-educated reflexes and Slippers' momentary indecision.

Obviously the dapper man had considered that the young Texan posed the greater and more immediate threat to his life. However, with his right forefinger commencing to tighten—the hammer was already cocked when the Remington had appeared—he saw and heard Silk open fire. For a vitally important split-second, Slippers wavered between which of his assailants he should deal with first.

Seeing his opportunity, the Kid took it by diving sideways and to the left. He had just—and only just—moved when Slippers' weapon spat. Its bullet passed where his body had been an instant before, ending its flight harmlessly in the wall.

Landing on his side, the Kid had completed his draw as he was going down. Lining the big Dragoon, he squeezed the trigger. Forty grains of black powder—an equivalent load to that fired by a Winchester Model of 1873 *rifle* and twelve grains *more* than his "old yellow boy" could handle—expelled a .44-caliber soft lead ball which ripped into Slippers' left shoulder.

Hurled bodily against the wall, the dapper man was badly injured and helpless—but that did not save him.

Silk's weapon, a British-made Webley Royal Irish Constabulary .450-caliber revolver with its barrel reduced to two inches and the lanyard ring removed from its butt as an aid to concealment, roared twice as fast as he could operate the double-action mechanism.

The striken man jerked under the impacts, as the bullets ploughed their way into his chest and through his heart. He was dead before his body struck the floor. Watching him go down, the Kid wondered what Marshal Anse Dale would say about the shooting. There was, he realized, also the danger that the peace officer might recognize Belle Starr or expose Belle Boyd as a fake.

CHAPTER TEN

He Knows I Killed His Nephew

"Hello down there," called the shorter of the two riders who sat their horses on the rim above where the Ysabel Kid and his party were setting up camp on the third night after their departure from San Antonio. "Can me 'n' my nephew come in?"

Contrary to the Kid's fears, Marshal Anse Dale had neither recognized Belle Starr nor exposed the Rebel Spy. On the peace officer's arrival at the Bon Ton Restaurant, the girls had kept in the background and allowed the Kid to make the explanations. He had told what was basically the truth. Omitting the fact that he and Silk had already known about the Frenchmen, he had stated that they were compelled to defend themselves when the pair had started to draw on them. There had been sufficent independent witnesses to corroborate the story without the need to involve either of the Belles. Nor had there been any difficulty in establishing a motive for the unprovoked attack. In fact, Dale himself had provided it.

The idler from the livery barn had been found murdered

earlier that afternoon. In the course of his investigation, the
marshal had discovered that—as he and the Kid had suspected—the victim had been hired, along with a man at every
other livery barn, to report on the arrival of any members of
the OD Connected. Having obtained a description of the men
who had done the hiring, Dale was satisfied that they were the
Kid's and Silk's victims. He had also assumed that, having
recognized the young Texan and been afraid it might be mutual,
the pair had tried to kill him and escape. So the marshal had
not pressed the matter any further, beyond asking pointedly
when the Kid would be leaving. He had been assured that the
departure would be in the near future and that to the best of
the young Texan's knowledge, there was not likely to be any
more trouble. Dale had said that he hoped there would not be.

Even without the marshal's hint that—due to the shooting—
he was not too popular in San Antonio, the Kid had already
realized that too long a stay would be inadvisable. Being equally
aware of the risk of meeting somebody who knew the real Betty
Hardin, Belle Boyd had turned the incident to their advantage.
On returning to the Sandford Hotel, she had suggested that—
as they disposed of both sets of watchers—it might be wise
to leave for *Casa* Serrano before any more could arrive.

Octavius Xavier Guillemot had seen the wisdom of making
an early departure. Asking Belle Starr how soon they could
leave, he had been told that it would be possible to go at sun-
up the following morning. Acting upon the instructions which
she had received at the start of her assignment from the "Pinkerton National Detective Agency," she had already hired a
buckboard, horses, supplies and had employed a leathery old
timer called Salt-Hoss to act as wrangler. Pointing out that
"Miss Hardin" would need a chaperone, the lady outlaw had
contrived to have herself included in the party. As the Rebel
Spy had wanted to find out why the other girl was so interested
in the affair, she had—pretending to be reluctant—allowed
the men to "persuade" her that it was for the best and had
agreed.

Learning that "Miss Hardin" had not yet arranged for any
accommodation, Starr had suggested that Boyd shared her room
at the hotel and the offer had been apparently grudgingly accepted. Ordered by the Rebel Spy to help collect her baggage,

the Kid had left with the girls and Silk had insisted upon accompanying them. Once out of the suite, the secretary had started to display gallantry towards and interest in "Miss Hardin." Hoping that it might be productive, Boyd had encouraged him to continue along those lines. However, no matter what might develop out of the situation in the future, Silk's presence had prevented the Rebel Spy and the Kid from satisfying their curiosity regarding the lady outlaw's behavior during the collection of the baggage.

That night, in the privacy of her room, Starr had been reasonably frank with Boyd. She had claimed that she had not betrayed the Rebel Spy or the Kid, who could not be present during the interview but was told of it later, because of their previous friendship.

Having settled that aspect satisfactorily, Starr had gone on to explain how Guillemot had hired her—through Ram Turtle—to do more than organize the transport for their journey to *Casa* Serrano and to discover the identities of the men who were following him. She was also to try and find out who had passed them the information that had set them on his trail, which had suggested he was not so certain as he had pretended to be regarding the guilt of his valet. Realizing that the most logical suspect was Silk, Boyd had understood why Starr had shown such disapproval when she had suggested the "lady detective" should attempt to learn the traitor's name. When dealing with a man who was a dangerous as the secretary had proved himself to be, it did not pay to take chances or to arouse his suspicions.

Either as evidence of her good faith, or to show that it could not be used as a lever against her, Starr had discussed her presence in Guillemot's suite during the Kid's first visit. Shortly before she had been hired by the Ox, Ehlring and Werra had asked Ram Turtle for advice on hiring gun-hands in the San Antonio area. Turtle had learned enough to suspect that they were involved with Guillemot. So Starr had seen a way in which she might obtain the information required by the Ox. She had been too late to prevent Werra from leaving Fort Worth, but with Turtle's help had been accepted as a useful contact by Ehlring. Although she had prevented the Kid from falling into the trap, she had failed in her main purpose. She had claimed—and Boyd believed her—that she had not known the identities of the Germans' victims.

However, after having been so forthcoming, Starr had been less so regarding her motives for accompanying the party. Her explanation—that she had been hired to do a job and wanted to see it through—had not been overconvincing. Seeing that the Rebel Spy was skeptical, she had admitted to being intrigued by the vast amount of interest which was being shown in Guillemot's activities. Being aware of his status in international criminal circles, she had decided that an investigation into them might be worthwhile. Like Boyd and the Kid, she had no idea of what made the recovery of the original Bowie knife so important; but had accepted that it must be very valuable for the Ox to be involved.

One thing Starr had refused to comment upon was how she would act if their mission was successful. Knowing that to continue to press that point would be futile, Boyd had let it drop. Nor had she been communicative regarding the United States' Secret Service taking so much notice of the affair. With other countries' agents involved, it was obvious that her department would want to find out why. Although a truce had been declared between them, the Rebel Spy had decided that— past friendship notwithstanding—she would have to keep a wary eye on the lady outlaw if the Ox achieved his purpose.

Setting off early the following morning, the party had headed south along the stagecoach trail which would eventually lead them to Eagle Pass and a ferry across the Rio Grande. While the girls rode horses, Guillemot and Silk—clad in clothes suitable for their pose as hunters—travelled in a buckboard which also carried their baggage. Leaving Salt-Hoss to handle the spare horses, the Kid had spent the day either behind or ahead of his companions. He had seen nothing to suggest that the Germans might have returned to San Antonio and were following, or were waiting along the trail for them to arrive with the intention of ambushing them.

The day had passed uneventfully and the night had been spent at the hotel in Hondo, seat of Medina County. Silk had continued to show great attention to "Miss Hardin," leaving Salt-Hoss and the hostler at the livery barn to deal with the buckboard's team and luggage so that he could help her unsaddle and care for her horse. From all appearances, Guillemot had not approved of his secretary's behavior towards the girl. Although he had not commented on the matter, the Kid had sensed that the Ox was perturbed by such a development.

During the evening, the Kid had sought to find out if anybody answering the two Germans' description had passed through the town. While the answers had been negative, he had remembered noticing the tracks of a buckboard leaving the trail about a mile from Hondo. At the time, he had thought nothing of them. However, in the light of a later discovery, he had considered it was possible that—wanting to avoid their presence being disclosed—they had gone around the town. He had located the place where the vehicle had rejoined the trail shortly after they had set off the following morning, but had decided against mentioning the matter to his companions.

The party had passed the second night at Uvalde. Once again, the Kid had found the tracks of the same buckboard leaving the trail at an angle which would keep its occupants out of sight of the town. So he had felt even more certain that it was carrying the Germans and guessed that, having anticipated the point at which the party would cross the Rio Grande, they were heading for Eagle Pass.

There had been little opportunity for the Kid to discuss his findings with Belle Boyd. Continuing to play her part as the snobbish, arrogant and spoiled "Betty Hardin," she had harrassed him to such an extent that it would have been highly suspicious for them to be seen indulging in a lengthy conversation. What was more, the opportunity to do so had been limited by Silk monopolizing so much of her time.

In one way, the latter aspect had been advantageous to the Rebel Spy and the Kid. Guillemot had started to show a growing interest in the young Texan's background and abilities. Most of the information had been supplied by Belle Starr and Salt-Hoss, the latter having known the Kid slightly and by reputation during the days when he and his father had ridden the border-smuggler trails. From them, the Ox had formed a fairly accurate idea of the young Texan's ability as a very capable and efficient fighting man. He had also learned that the Kid possessed considerable knowledge of the border country. That he was impressed had been obvious, also he appeared to have a reason for his curiosity. On the second night, after the Ox had gone to bed and Boyd was seated elsewhere with Silk, Starr had told the Kid that she had been asked to sound out the extent of his loyalty to the OD Connected.

While the Kid had felt sure that the Germans would refrain from taking any action until after the party was in Mexico, he had decided against taking chances. So, on the pretext that to do so would shorten their journey and give them an opportunity to obtain practical experience which would prove useful once they had crossed the Rio Grande, he had suggested that they should go directly to Eagle Pass instead of following the trail via Crystal City in Zavala County.

Accepting the Kid's suggestion, the party had realized that they would be compelled to spend the night out of doors. However, as doing so would be the rule rather than the exception during the journey from the border to *Casa* Serrano and back, they had all agreed that it would do them no harm to start becoming accustomed to such conditions.

Scouting ahead of his companions in the late afternoon, the Kid had selected a suitable campsite for the party. In a valley which would offer shelter from the elements if the weather should take a turn for the worse, on the banks of a stream that offered grazing for the horses and water to satisfy all their needs, it was a pleasant location. They had made most of their preparations for the night when the two riders had appeared on the rim.

"How about it, Mr. Guillemot?" the Kid inquired, without either raising or lowering the rifle which he had picked up on hearing the horses approaching. "It'd be's well to find out who they are and what they're doing hereabouts."

"I agree," the Ox replied, before any of the others could speak. "But there's probably nothing to worry about."

"Nope," the Kid drawled. "They're likely just a couple of cowhands wanting to pass the time of day and have a meal." He raised his voice and went on, "Come ahead, gents!"

For all his casual words, the Kid subjected the riders to a careful scrutiny as they came down the slope. They and their horses—a big blue roan and an equally large, powerful iron-grey—showed signs to his range-wise eyes of having been travelling hard very recently. What was more, for all his comment to Guillemot, the Kid suspected that they were something other than merely chance-passing cowhands. The way in which they had studied their back trail before commencing the descent into the valley had given a warning of that.

One was of medium height, in his mid-thirties, with a sun-reddened face of almost cherubic appearance. He had thinning, curly brown hair and gave an impression of being corpulent. A white "planter's" hat sat on the back of his head. He had on a fringed buckskin jacket, open-necked blue shirt with a matching bandana, Levi's pants and low-heeled boots. While there was a Winchester rifle in his saddleboot, he neither wore a gunbelt nor showed signs of being armed in any other way.

Topping the six foot level by maybe two inches, the second man looked to be in his very early twenties. He had wide shoulders and a lean waist, being clad—with the exception of a black J. B. Stetson hat—in the same general fashion as his companion. Rusty-red hair topped a face which, despite a badly broken nose, a scar over the left eye-brow and a thickened left ear, was ruggedly handsome. He too had a Winchester in his saddleboot and was carrying in the low-tied, fast-draw holster of his gunbelt a Colt 1860 Army revolver that had been re-chambered so that it would fire metallic cartridges.

Bringing their horses to a halt, the newcomers sat for a moment looking at the members of the party. There was, however, nothing hostile in the scrutiny.

"Sorry about barging in on you-all like this, folks," the smaller man announced in a pleasant and amicable voice. He swung from his saddle and left the blue roan standing ground hitched by its dangling reins. "The name's Brady Anchor and this here's my nephew, Jefferson Trade."[1]

"Good evening, gentlemen," Guillemot acknowledged, rising from the trunk upon which he had been seated since its removal from the backboard. "I trust that you will join us for supper?"

"That's right neighborly of you, sir," Brady Anchor declared. "We got some victuals—"

"They won't be needed," Guillemot assured him. "We have

1. Brady Anchor and Jefferson Trade had made some changes to their armament by the time they became involved in the incidents recorded in: *Two Miles to the Border*.

more than sufficient, if the ladies don't object to the little extra work."

"*Gracias,*" Brady drawled. "That being the case, we'll lend a hand to 'tend to your hosses."

"Ysabel!" Belle Boyd called, adopting her usual tone. "Go and collect some wood, then make a fire."

"Sure, *Miss Hardin,*" the Kid answered, scowling as if angry at the way in which she had addressed him before the newcomers.

"I'll come with you," Brady suggested as the young Texan turned away. "You help the gent with the stock, Jefferson."

"Yo!" Jefferson Trade responded.

"Way you was holding that old yellow boy's we rode up," Brady remarked in conversational tones, after the Kid had placed his rifle on the buckboard's seat and they were walking towards the nearby trees in search of firewood, "I'd say you could be expecting trouble."

"Not more'n mostly," the youngster replied.

"You wouldn't have done nothing to get Juan Escuchador riled up at you then?" Brady inquired.

"Would you have call to think's I might?" the Kid countered, letting his right hand drift in a casual-seeming fashion towards the butt of the old Dragoon Colt.

Having made a closer examination of the stocky man as they were walking, the Kid had drawn further conclusions. What appeared to be corpulence was merely the effect caused by the clothing, he had decided. Under the garments lay a hard and powerful body, for the man walked with a rubbery bounce which did not go with a load of fat. In addition, there was a distinct—if unobtrusive—bulge below his *right* armpit that suggested he might be carrying a weapon concealed beneath his jacket.

"Not so much me's Marshal Dale from back to San Antonio," Brady replied, giving no hint that he had noticed the motions of the Kid's hand although the young Texan did not doubt that he had. He reached with his right hand into the jacket's left breast pocket. "Gave me this letter to show's he'd asked me 'n' my nephew to drift down this way and tell you's Escuchador's looking for you."

Accepting the envelope, the Kid extracted and read the letter:

"Lon,

Rosa Rio's sent word that Juan Escuchador is gunning for you. The man who is bringing this is Brady Anchor. He knows as much as I do and you can trust him and his nephew like you would me.

Yours faithfully,
Anse Dale."

"Me 'n' my nephew'd just dropped by to say 'howdy' to the marshal, us being old friends," the stocky man explained, when the Kid turned a quizzical glance at him. "One of Rosa Rio's bouncers came in and asked where you might be. When Anse said you'd left town, the feller asked him to send somebody after you and say that she hadn't sent Juan Escuchador on your trail, nor told him nothing. That was all the feller would, or could—which comes out the same way—tell. Anyways, Anse told me who you was and asked if I'd come by to give you the word."

"I'm much obliged," the Kid declared, folding the letter and returning it to the envelope.

"Escuchador's one bad *hombre,*" Brady warned. "Has he got something against you personal, or against those folks you're travelling with."

"Just me," the Kid replied. "I reckon he knows I killed his nephew."

"Whee-dogie!" Brady breathed, although the Kid guessed that Marshal Dale had already supplied that information. "He's not going to take kindly to it. You're lucky in one way, though. He's only got half a dozen men at his back."

"You've seen 'em, huh?"

"Passed 'em early this morning. We circled 'n' got ahead of 'em without being seen. Found where you'd turned off and followed, but not close enough to your tracks for our sign to be seen."

"Maybe they're figuring that we'll stick to the trail," the Kid suggested.

"I wouldn't count on it, because they haven't," Brady answered. "They turned off where you did. Maybe they won't have caught up by nightfall, but they'll not be far behind and you sure's hell can't lick 'em to Eagle Pass. They'll be on to you afore then."

CHAPTER ELEVEN

I'll Stand By Mr. Ysabel

Having collected wood and returned to the rest of the party, the Ysabel Kid told them the news which Brady Anchor and Jefferson Trade had brought from San Antonio de Bexar. As he was speaking, he watched his companions' faces to see how they were reacting to what he was saying.

Seated on the trunk, Octavius Xavier Guillemot frowned and glanced to where a Sharps "Old Reliable" buffalo gun— which he had brought from the East as an aid to his pose as a hunter and had already proved that he could use with some skill by shooting a deer at long range on the second day of the journey—leaned against the buckboard. Although he swung his bland, emotionless face back towards the Kid, he did not offer any comment.

Belle Boyd and Belle Starr stood just as quietly, although they showed that they appreciated the gravity of the situation. While neither of them was wearing the gunbelt and revolver which the Kid knew each was carrying in her travelling bags, they both had a Winchester Model of 1866 carbine in their saddleboots. He knew that they were capable of using the weapons. However, they too did not speak. Both appeared to be waiting for somebody else to open the conversation.

Spitting out a spurt of tobacco juice, Salt-Hoss dropped a gnarled right hand to the butt of his holstered Colt 1860 Army revolver. Then he began to scrutinize the rim down which they had come.

Standing near to Belle Boyd, as had become his usual habit, Anthony Silk looked briefly at her. While clad in a light colored, thin suit and wearing his gunbelt, he still retained the Webley in what the Kid now knew to be a split-fronted, spring-retention shoulder holster. Being aware of the secretary's continued, thinly veiled, hostility, the young Texan did not doubt that he would try to turn the situation to his advantage.

"This Mexican is after *you*, Ysabel," Silk stated, a calculating glint coming into his eyes.

"He's after me," the Kid conceded, guessing what was coming.

So did the rest of the party, if the way they were watching Silk was anything to go by.

"In which case," the secretary continued, his left hand rising to stroke at the jacket's lapel, "he has no quarrel with the rest of us."

"*You* might say that," the Kid said quietly.

"So if you leave now, when he arrives we can tell him that you've gone," Silk explained, selecting his words with care. He wanted "Miss Hardin" to believe that, although his primary concern was for herself and the others, he was also thinking of her "grandfather's" employee whom she had told him was regarded as being of considerable use around the ranch. So he continued, "By the time he gets here, you'll be too far away for him to catch you. But he'll leave us alone and go after you."

"I wouldn't want to count too hard on that, was I you, mister," Brady Anchor warned, from where he was standing alongside his nephew. "Escuchador's just about's mean and ornery a *bandido* as ever slit a throat. No matter what you told him, him and his boys'd praise the Saints for giving 'em such good pickings as they was gunning you down."

"They'd kill *you* quick, mister," Jefferson Trade supplemented. "Only with the ladies, it wouldn't likely be so quick—although they soon enough get 'round to wishing it had been, what'd happen to 'em."

"I'll go along with Brady and Jeff on that," Belle Starr declared, glaring coldly at Silk. "Good as you are with a gun, you couldn't handle seven like Escuchador's gang. I don't know about Miss Hardin, but much as I'd hate to be killed, I'd hate even worse to be taken alive by them."

"I agree with Miss Beauregard," Belle Boyd went on, with the air of conveying a favor to the other girl by even considering her opinion. Then she continued in her current haughty fashion, "If I thought that it would do any good, I'd send Ysabel home straight away. But, from what I know about Mexicans, they wouldn't just ride off after him and leave such valuable loot as our belongings would be."

"I was only thinking of *you*, Miss Hardin!" the secretary assured her hurriedly, but he was clearly annoyed by the dismissal of his suggestion. "If you weren't with us, I wouldn't have said that he should go. But if there's going to be shooting—"

"I've never been one for billing in on something that isn't rightly any of my never-mind, mister," Brad Anchor injected, with every evidence of politeness and apology for his lapse. Refusing to be silenced by the glowering look which Silk directed at him, he went on, "But there'll be shooting whether the Kid goes or stays."

"I don't suppose that we could buy him off, could we?" Guillemot inquired, studying the stocky, cherubic-looking man with interest and appraisal.

"Nope," Brady replied. "Even if he let you make the offer—"

"We could be waiting, with our weapons ready," Silk interrupted, "so that he'd rather listen than chance being shot."

"You *could*," Brady admitted, but showed that he had reservations regarding the idea. "Only he'd gun you down after he'd taken your money. If he didn't do it straight away, he cut ahead and bushwhack you. Escuchador's never been one for taking less than all he can get when all that's standing between him and it are a few killings."

"You say that they're some way behind, Mr. Anchor?" Guillemot asked, rubbing at his multiple chins with an enormous hand.

"Two-three miles back and not a-rushing," the stocky man agreed. "But coming for all of that."

"Then we could start moving and outrun them to Eagle Pass," the Ox suggested. "They're hardly likely to dare follow us into a town, are they?"

"Nope," Brady conceded. "Trouble being, you'd never make it. They can travel a whole heap faster on horseback than you'll be able to do with your rig, especially after it gets dark."

"Damn it!" Silk ejaculated, glaring at the Indian-dark young Texan. He had noticed how the others were exchanging perturbed glances, which told of their understanding of the precarious nature of their predicament, and saw in it a way of reducing his employer's regard for the man who was responsible for it. "If you hadn't killed his nephew, none of this would be happening."

"Likely," the Kid answered, so quietly and mildly that anybody who knew him would have taken a warning from his tones. "Only it seemed the reasonable thing to do at the time, him being set on killing Dusty and me. 'Specially seeing's how he was trying to stop us coming to help your boss."

"We can hardly blame Mr. Ysabel for defending himself, Silk," Guillemot supplemented. "And talking about what should, or shouldn't, have happened isn't going to get us anywhere. Our problem is to decide what to do for the best."

"I've got some notions on *that*," the Kid declared, standing on spread-apart feet and with his right hand turned palm-outwards *very* close to the butt of the old Dragoon Colt. Taken with the challenging way in which he was looking at the secretary, it was a provocative posture. "And so has Mr. Silk—happen he'd like to spit 'em out."

"I don't want to see Miss Hardin endangered—" the secretary began sullenly.

"Nor do any of us," Guillemot put in, standing up. "I think *that* goes without saying. However, I'm satisfied that asking Mr. Ysabel to leave won't achieve anything."

"Then what do we do?" Silk demanded.

"Suppose we ask somebody who *knows* just how serious the situation is?" the Ox answered, but the way in which he was speaking showed—particularly to his secretary, who had come to know him very well—that he was giving an order. "After all I've seen of him, I'll stand by Mr. Ysabel and do whatever he thinks will be best."

"Well, sir," the Kid drawled, ignoring Silk's angry hiss and obvious disapproval. "First off, I'd say offer Brady and Jeff maybe fifty dollars a-piece to stay with us for a spell."

"*Fifty dollars each!*" Silk spat out. "You're damned free with our money."

"I didn't know it was *your* money, mister," the Kid answered, looking relaxed despite being ready to spring into instant motion if he had pushed the secretary too far. "But if—"

"I think that I'm quite capable of deciding how to spend *my* money, Silk," Guillemot interjected coldly, before the other could make any response. "Do you know these gentlemen, Mr. Ysabel?"

"Nope, not per—" the Kid admitted, but was not allowed to continue.

"How did you get involved in this?" Silk demanded, scowling at the newcomers.

"I don't know's how we are involved in it, mister," Brady Anchor replied. "We were Anse Dale's deputies three years back. When he heard we was headed down Zavala County way, he asked us to drop by and warn you folks about Escuchador. Which's what we've done and, having done it, we'll be moving on."

"Just a moment, Mr. Anchor," Guillemot boomed. "I think Mr. Ysabel was going to say something more."

"Why sure," the Kid agreed, darting a triumphant glance at Silk. "Happen these gents're the same Brady Anchor 'n' Jefferson Trade's worked for Colin Farquharson on the Upper Nueces early last year, they'd be good men to have around."

"We worked for Colin," Brady conceded. "Only it was on the Middle San Saba. Which means you're testing us, or don't know as much's you let on."

"Colin allowed you was left-handed, Brady," the Kid replied

with a grin. "And that you tote your gun in the damnedest rig he'd ever seen. In a shoulder-holster that hangs cross-wise instead of down."

"Like this?" Brady inquired, drawing open the right side of his jacket to show that his holster was suspended horizontally instead of the more usual vertical.

"Just like that," the Kid confirmed. "No offence meant, Brady, Jeff."

"None took, Kid," Brady assured him and Jefferson Trade muttered agreement.

"You can rely upon them, Mr. Guillemot," Belle Boyd announced, concealing her satisfaction at the way the Kid was playing Guillemot against Silk. It would help her own efforts with the secretary. "Colin has always spoken highly of them."

"Very well, Miss Hardin," the Ox replied and looked at the newcomers. "As you have been deputies, that suggests you have considerable proficiency with your weapons."

"We both know which end the lead goes in and where it comes out," Brady confessed off-handedly. "And, happen what we're shooting at's stood still and's big enough, we can most times hit what we're aiming at."

"Only if it's real close," Jeffer supplemented.

"I think you're being modest," Guillemot smiled. "May I ask if you are going to Zavala County on a matter of urgency?"

"Not especially," Brady admitted.

"Would it be taking you out of your way to come to Eagle Pass with us?" the Ox went on. "I'd be willing to reimburse you."

"We'd rather get paid," Jefferson stated. "See, mister, we're just a couple of lil ole country boys who're trying to make enough money to live in a manner we've always been too poor to get accustomed to."

"And you would advise that I hire them to join us, Mr. Ysabel?" Guillemot asked.

"I reckon you'd be making right good sense," the Kid confirmed.

"Very well," Guillemot said, taking no notice of Silk's obvious disapproval. "I'll pay you fifty dollars each to accompany us to Eagle Pass, gentlemen."

Watching the men, Belle was delighted by the further evidence that Silk hated the way in which Guillemot was showing preference for the Kid's judgement. She had sensed from the beginning that the "secretary" was dissatisfied with his subordinate's capacity and now saw a threat to it in the way the Ox was treating the young Texan. That was, she supposed, why Silk had started to cultivate "Betty Hardin." He hoped to use her as the means of improving his situation. So she had been playing him along with the intention of discovering if he knew why Guillemot was going to so much trouble and expense to obtain James Bowie's knife. From the scowl on Silk's face, she believed that he might be receptive to sympathy and, as a result of receiving it, could possibly be persuaded to divulge at least some of the required information.

Always providing, Belle told herself, that the Mexicans could be prevented from interfering. She did not underestimate the threat which Escuchador was posing to all their lives. However, she felt sure that the Kid would be able to supply a solution to the problem. If he did, he would strengthen his position with Guillemot and render Silk even more susceptible to her wishes.

"Sir," Brady drawled. "You've just hired yourself two men."

"One thing, though," the Kid drawled, before any more could be said. "For that kind of money, I'd say you ought to be willing to do something a mite harder than just riding along with us to Eagle Pass and collecting it."

"I don't understand—" Guillemot began, showing that he was puzzled.

"Escuchador's no fool," the Kid elaborated. "He's not about to try anything when he sees we've got two extra men riding along. He'll just follow until after they pull out and then jump us."

"Are you suggesting that we should hire them to come all the way to *Casa*—where we are going?" Guillemot asked.

"Well, no sir," the Kid replied. "That wasn't exactly what I had in mind."

"Then what—!" the Ox commenced.

"Hey, Salt-Hoss," the Kid interrupted, glancing at the old timer. "How's about lighting up a fire so's the ladies can make us a meal?"

"A *fire!*" Silk snorted, certain that his rival was committing an incredibly stupid blunder which would convince Guillemot that he was of no use as an ally. "If we do *that*, the smoke will tell the Mexicans where we are."

"Well I'm damned!" the Kid ejaculated, sounding exasperated as he slapped his left thigh with his near hand. "I just hadn't thought it'd do *that!*"

"Hello the fire!" called a voice from the fringe of the post oak trees that surrounded the clearing in which Juan Escuchador and his gang had camped for the night. "Can I come on in and share it?"

Every man in the villainous-looking group gathered around the fire had already heard the rider as he had come from the northeast. However, at the evidence that he was approaching their location, they started to reach for holstered revolvers or the various rifles which were leaning against their saddles.

"No shooting!" the burly, brutal-featured and best-dressed member of the party commanded. "We're too close to where *Cabrito's* camping and he doesn't know we're around. Let this feller come in, then one of you can use your knife.

"*Si*, Juan," responded one of the gang, relaxing, and the rest muttered their concurrence as they also settled down to either sit or squat on their haunches.

"Come ahead, *amigo*," Juan Escuchador called, standing up. He glared as some of his companions sought to emulate his example and resumed speaking in their native tongue after having addressed an invitation in English. "Stay down there, damn you. Don't do anything to scare him off."

Obeying their leader's command, the Mexicans remained in passive postures. Their saddles and bed rolls were set out for the night and their horses were either picketed or hobbled around the clearing. All of them peered with considerable interest at the rider who was approaching. Sufficient moonlight was filtering through the trees for them to make out various details of his appearance.

If his voice had been any guide, the man riding towards the clearing was a Texan. Tall, slim, seated on a big, dark-colored horse, he had on a fringed buckskin jacket, ooen-necked white shirt, multi-hued bandana and Levi's pants. However, the brim of his white "planter's" hat threw a shadow which obscured his features. A gunbelt was strapped about his lean waist, but the jacket prevented the Mexicans from seeing the kind of weapons it was supporting. However, he kept both of his hands in plain sight and did nothing to make them suspicious.

On coming to the fringe of the area illuminated by the fire, the newcomer reined his horse so that it halted with its right side towards the Mexicans. Still acting in a casual manner, although without allowing them to see his face, he dismounted with the animal between himself and them. Having done so, he gave its rump a slap with his right hand and it walked forward. As he came into full length view once more, he proved to have a Winchester rifle in his hands and, advancing a couple of paces, he allowed them to take their first unimpeded sight of his young-looking, Indian-dark face.

"Howdy, *Senor* Escuchador," the Texan greeted in fluent Spanish. "I hear that you're looking for me."

"*Cabrito?*" Escuchador gasped and his right hand started to move towards the butt of the low-tied Colt Civilian Model Peacemaker that he was wearing.

"Easy, all of you!" the Ysabel Kid commanded and, although his left hand was grasping the wrist of the butt—with his right holding the foregrip—he lined the rifle at waist level with deft and practiced ease. "That's right. I'm *Cabrito*."

Watching the Winchester's muzzle swinging in an arc which encompassed them all, the men carried out the order which the Kid had given. They were all too aware of *Cabrito's*—as Mexicans translated "Kid"—deadly skill with such a weapon and doubted if handling it left-handed would make him much less effective.

"Now that's a lot better," the Kid went on, still employing the kind of Spanish which the *bandidos* could understand. "It'll let me tell you what happened to your nephew, *Senor* Escuchador."

"How did you know what I was after you for?" Escuchador demanded, having moved his hand well clear of the holstered revolver.

"It figured," the Kid answered and his voice hardened as he went on to prove that he was keeping *all* of the group under observation. "Just like it figures that *hombre* with the scar's going to be scratching himself near his gun with a hole in his head, happen he don't quit doing it."

"Stop that, damn you!" Escuchador commanded, glaring at the man in question, although he had not needed to give the order as it had already been anticipated. "Go on, *Cabrito.*"

"Feller you should be all riled up about is Matteo Urizza," the Kid obliged. "It was him who brought your nephew after us, only he didn't let on it was Dusty Fog and me they'd be going up against."

"Just the *two* of you?" Escuchador asked.

"Did Matt allow there was more?" the Kid inquired, turning the Winchester's barrel slightly and allowing his tone to take on the menacing timber again. "Damn it, Juan, I've never seen such a bunch for fidgeting and fussing near their guns. It's making me so nervous, I swear I'll shoot next time—regardless of who I'm lining up on when it happens."

"Sit still, all of you!" Escuchador snarled, taking *very* careful notice of the way that the rifle had halted so that it was lined on his chest. He understood the Kid's meaning all too well and continued in a milder voice. "I'm sorry about that, *Cabrito,* only you've got them jumpy coming in like you did."

"I figured it'd be best done that way, so's we'd get a chance to talk things out peaceable instead of throwing lead," the Kid drawled. "Thing that worried me was Matt might've told you I wasn't wearing my usual clothes and am riding the Appaloosa."

"There was a lot Urizza didn't tell me, it seems," Escuchador gritted. "He said that a whole bunch of you jumped him and Enrique for no reason."

"Well now," the Kid replied. "That's not exactly the way it happened. Dusty and I were riding along, wasn't anybody else with us, when Enrique came up from behind a rock and started to throw down on us. Urizza didn't show at all. He lit out just after your nephew died, without even trying to burn lead."

"*Hijo de puta!*" Escuchador spat out furiously.

"I allus figured that's what his mother must have been," the Kid commented, knowing that the expression meant "son of a whore." Then he went on with such sincerity that he might have been speaking the truth, "Enrique wasn't quite dead when we got to him and he was some surprised when he learned who he'd been up against. Seemed like Urizza had forgotten to tell him."

"And I let the bastard ride off!" Escuchador spluttered.

"I just bet he told you I was headed down to San Antonio on my lonesome," the Kid continued. "Was figuring after all the lies he'd told you, you'd come gunning for me. Which's what he wanted, having took pay to get me but being scared to try again. Point being, Juan, I'm right sorry about what happened. But when Enrique come up shooting, there wasn't anything else I could do but cut loose back at him."

"That's understandable," Escuchador conceded.

"And, seeing you fellers coming," the Kid went on, "I could guess what you had in mind. So I figured I'd best drop by, explain and try to save us all a heap of grief. If I hadn't and you boys had tried to jump us tomorrow like you planned"— he could see that he had guessed correctly—"there'd have been some of you dead when the smoke cleared." Watching the Mexicans, he could see that he had made a telling point and elaborated upon it. "I know it's hard on you, Juan, losing your nephew and all, and how you'd want to try to avenge him, way you was told it happened. But is it worth getting some of these fellers killed over now you know the truth?"

"Is it hell," Escuchador declared, having glanced at his men and decided that they expected such a response. "I had to try to do something, you know that, *Cabrito.*"

"I'm not holding it against you," the Kid assured him. "Just as long as you don't keep on with it."

"I won't," Escuchador promised. "Hell, he only got to be my kin because some *gringo* priest took a fancy to my sister Maria and sired him one night after confession. Now you've explained, I can tell her why I didn't try to avenge him."

"Bueno," the Kid drawled, lowering the muzzle of his rifle out of alignment. "I'm right pleased it's been settled peaceable and I'll be on my way."

"Why not stop for a meal?" Escuchador offered.

"I'd like to, only I've got one waiting for me when I get back to our camp," the Kid replied. "Which *isn't* where you saw the smoke coming up."

"You're a crafty son-of-a-gun," Escuchador chuckled.

"How about a cup of coffee before you go?"

"I'd like to, but it's the boss lady who's cooked the meal and she'll get riled happen I let it get cold," the Kid answered. "*Adios*, Juan, *amigos*, I'm real pleased things've worked out right and peaceful between us."

With that, the young Texan turned on his heel. Before he had taken his second step, Escuchador reached towards the butt of the holstered Colt. Clearly his men had been expecting some such action in spite of the way the conversation had progressed. Every one began to grab for a weapon and started to rise.

CHAPTER TWELVE

You Could Get The Kid Killed

"You did realize that I was only thinking of *you* when I suggested that the half-breed should clear out this evening, didn't you, Miss Hardin?" Anthony Silk asked earnestly, taking the opportunity which had been presented to him for a private conversation with the girl.

"Of course I did," the Rebel Spy assured him, having hoped for such a development when bringing him a cup of coffee from the camp. "And I feel much safer with *you* up here keeping watch."

"It wasn't that I minded doing this," Silk insisted, wanting to clear away any ideas that the girl might be harbouring to the contrary. "I just didn't care for the way that damned half-breed was giving orders."

"Mr. Guillemot seemed to approve of them," Belle pointed out, controlling the irritation she was experiencing over the secretary's references to the Ysabel Kid's mixed blood and selecting a comment which she felt sure would add fuel to his sense of discontent.

"He did," Silk gritted, gripping the cup tighter and moving restlessly as he remembered how he had failed to discredit the young Texan.

Despite the Kid's comment when Silk had warned him about the danger of lighting a fire, he had gone on to show that it might not have been such a foolish suggestion after all. He had claimed that, knowing with whom they were dealing, the Mexican *bandidos* would be disinclined to chance an attack in the darkness. Once they had seen the smoke rising, they would make camp themselves—selecting a spot from which the glow or smoke of their own fire would not be seen—and wait until the next day. As Brady Anchor and Jefferson Trade had agreed with the Kid's summation, Guillemot had gone along with the line of action which the young Texan had proposed.

While the Kid had been pretty certain that Juan Escuchador would hold off until the following morning at least, preferring to catch the party on the move, he had suggested that precautions should be taken during his absence. One of them, which Silk had disputed, was that he should stand guard on the uppermost edge of a clump of bushes overlooking their camp. Much to the secretary's annoyance, Guillemot had once again backed up the young Texan and had insisted upon the order being obeyed.

Having decided that the rift between Guillemot and Silk might offer possibilities, Belle had waited for what she believed would be a good time to set about exploiting them. Allowing the disgruntled secretary almost three hours in which to brood alone on his grievances, she had brought him a cup of coffee. From the way in which the conversation was going, she sensed that it might possibly shed some light upon the mystery she was trying to solve.

"I can't say that I approved of how Ysabel was behaving," Belle declared, letting a note of haughty indignation creep into her voice. Showing a keen grasp of the situation, the Kid had given her orders so that she could pretend to resent and object to them. "He's already acting above his station. And if he brings this off, Mr. Guillemot is going to keep on listening to his suggestions. You and I might not have been here for all the notice he took of our opinions."

"Your grandfather sent him to act as our guide," Silk pointed

out, glancing at the bushes to make sure that he and the girl
could not been seen from the camp. Satisfied that they could
not, he looked along the bushes without seeing any sign of
"Magnolia Beauregard" who was keeping watch from the other
end.

"Yes," Belle Boyd agreed. "But *not* to take charge as he's
doing. Guillemot certainly seems impressed by him. Look at
the way he let himself be persuaded to hire those two men in
spite of your comments."

Although Silk sucked in a deep breath, he did not comment
on the girl's statement. So she too stood silent, allowing him
to consider the implications of what she had said.

"You know, Anthony—" Belle began, after almost a minute
had passed. "You don't mind if I call you Anthony when we're
alone, do you?"

"No," Silk answered, jolted from his reverie.

"And you can call me 'Betty,'" the girl instructed. "You
know, Anthony, I'm puzzled—"

"What about?" Silk wanted to know.

"Mr. Guillemot is going to a lot of trouble and expense to
collect the knife for the Bowie family," Belle remarked, watching his face.

"They're paying for it," Silk reminded her.

"I don't doubt that. But Mr. Guillemot doesn't strike me
as the kind of a man who would make such a long and un-
comfortable journey just to collect a knife for somebody else.
Surely he could have let you fetch it for him. You could have
made much better time on horseback than it's possible to do
with him riding the buckboard. And, after all, you *were* his
'strong right arm' I think he called you."

"He likes to handle things personally," Silk said coldly,
showing that he had taken notice of the way she had emphasized
the word "were."

"Obviously," Belle sniffed. "One might almost think that
the knife is so valuable that he doesn't trust even his 'strong
right arm' to collect it for him. Yet I don't see how it *could*
be. Possibly it might have a certain value as a trophy, but that
hardly warrants so many men having been hired to try to get
it."

Instead of replying, Silk studied the girl's beautiful face for

several seconds. A keen student of human—especially feminine—nature, he had already come to revise his original
impression that she was a somewhat naïve, if spoiled, arrogant
and self-opinionated snob who would fall easily under the spell
of his sophisticated charm. During their acquaintance, he had
decided that she was far more intelligent and worldly than he
had at first imagined. The way that the conversation was pro-
gressing gave him a hint that she suspected Guillemot of having
an ulterior motive for collecting the knife. Silk wondered if the
time had come for him to carry out the intentions towards which
he had been working since leaving San Antonio. However, his
plan might need to be changed in the light of the latest development. "Betty Hardin" might not be the dupe that he had
envisaged and hoped for.

Silk did not know the whole secret of Bowie's knife, but
he had learned sufficient to realize that he would need powerful
financial backing to utilize its full potential. Meeting "Betty
Hardin" had seemed to offer the means by which he could
obtain it; and from a source that was ideally suited to make the
most of it. Not only was her "grandfather" a very wealthy man,
but he also wielded considerable political influence in Texas.
The latter would be of tremendous importance. So Silk had
been hoping to use the girl to attain the General's confidence.

While satisfied on those points, Silk was wondering if the
time was right for a disclosure of his knowledge. He was aware
of how dangerous double-crossing the Ox would be. Certainly
he would never dare return to Europe once he had done so.
However, he wanted to be sure of the girl before he shared his
knowledge with her.

"That's true," Silk finally admitted, trying to sound as if
the idea had not occurred to him.

"And if it *is* so valuable," Belle went on, "perhaps Mr.
Guillemot doesn't intend to return it to the Bowie family."

"Maybe he doesn't," Silk answered non-committally.

"In which case, Ysabel would be of great use to him," Belle
continued. "Knowing that the men are after him, or will be
waiting when he returns, he might intend to avoid going back."

"How do you mean?" Silk challenged.

"Haven't you noticed the interest he's been showing in
Ysabel's knowledge of Mexico?" Belle demanded. "It could

be because he's hoping to go to the coast and take a ship, instead of returning to the United States."

"He wouldn't need Ysabel for that," Silk growled, but his voice showed uncertainty. "All we'd have to do would be return to the Rio Grande and follow it to the coast."

"Through some of the worst *bandido* and cut-throat infested country that you'll ever see?" Belle challenged. "*You* couldn't do it, Anthony, but Ysabel could. And I think Guillemot knows it."

"He can't do without *me!*" Silk growled, but it was obvious to the girl that he was trying to convince himself as much as her.

"He seems to have been doing so recently," Belle pointed out. "Look, Anthony, I don't pretend to know what makes the knife so valuable, although I'm sure that *you* do. What I do know is that Guillemot can't get it without my help and, if I had a better idea what it's all about, well, I could make up my mind what to do."

"How do you mean?"

"*Senor* Serrano will be doing the favor for the General, not the Bowie family, if he hands over the knife."

"So?" Silk prompted and, try as he might, he could not entirely restrain his eagerness.

"So, if it would be worth the General's while, I could suggest that Serrano sends it to him for disposal," Belle suggested. "And, if it is so valuable—"

"It is," Silk assured her.

"Why?" Belle asked and felt sure that she would be told what she wanted to know.

Before Silk could reply, they heard shots from the northeast—the direction in which Jefferson Trade, who had been sent to investigate, had claimed that the *bandidos* were bedding down for the night.

"It looks like the half-breed didn't manage to talk the Mexicans out of killing him," Silk remarked, not without a suggestion of satisfaction. "You'd better go back to the buckboard in case they come after us."

"But—!" Belle began, fighting down her concern for the Kid's welfare.

"Do it. You'll be safer down there," Silk ordered. "I'll stay and keep a watch in case they come."

"Very well," Belle replied, accepting that she would not receive any further information at that moment; but knowing she had implanted the seeds of doubt in Silk's head and that they might provide the required results in the future. "Take care of yourself, Anthony," she continued, stepping closer and kissing him lightly on the cheek. "I wouldn't want any harm to come to you."

With that, the Rebel Spy began to back away. She went slowly, watching Silk turn and stare to the northeast. The shooting had ended, but they had no way of knowing what the result might have been.

"Hard luck, 'Miss Hardin,' " Belle Starr's voice remarked quietly from the bushes as the other girl was passing the lower fringe of them on her way back to the camp. "You were handling it real well. Of course, the way you were doing it, you could get the Kid killed—unless Escuchador's already done it."

"Turn!" a voice shouted from the darkness as Escuchador started to draw his gun.

Not only the *bandidos* had expected their leader to behave in such a treacherous fashion.

Although the Ysabel Kid had told the other members of his party that he hoped to explain about Enrique Escuchador's death, he had realized that the chances of it doing any good were almost non-existent. So he had taken precautions. While he had approached the gang openly from the opposite direction to where his companions were camping, Brady Anchor and Jefferson Trade had been taking advantage of the distraction which he was providing. Having left their horses some distance away, with Salt-Hoss present to keep the animals quiet, they had moved in on foot.

Hearing the not unexpected warning, the Kid responded like lightning. Swivelling to his right, as being the shorter distance for his Winchester to move into alignment, he discovered that—in spite of his precaution—he was still in very serious peril. Already Escuchador's revolver was close to clearing the lip of its holster and, grabbing for weapons, the rest of the

Mexicans were coming to their feet as swiftly as they could manage.

Aiming by instinctive alignment, with the Winchester still at waist-level, the Kid began to fire as fast as he could operate the lever and produced the three shots per second which the manufacturer's advertisements claimed was possible. He swung the barrel as he did so, pouring a fan of flying lead in Escuchador's direction.

Shock twisted momentarily across the *bandido's* face as he realized that his trick had failed. Then the Kid's fourth, fifth and sixth bullets tore through his chest and flung him backwards to collide with one of his men.

Selecting the Mexican who was moving fastest and so posed the most immediate threat to the Kid's well-being, Brady Anchor—who had delivered the one-word warning—sighted and fired his Winchester, directing its bullet with deadly effect. Even as the *bandido,* hit in the head, twirled around and fell, Jefferson Trade displayed a comparable accuracy by tumbling the next swiftest in an equally lifeless heap. Then the two Texans turned their respective attention to the other Mexicans.

Although the remainder of the gang must have realized just how small were their chances of surviving, none of them offered to surrender. Only one of them escaped.

Having contrived to stay on his feet, the man who had been struck by Escuchador's body made no attempt to duplicate the actions of his companions. While they tried to bring their weapons into use, he let his fall and spun on his heel. Alarmed by the shooting, the horses were rearing and plunging. Darting to where one had contrived to tear free its picket-rope, he managed to vault astride its bare back and to cling on as it dashed away into the darkness. Only one of the men he had deserted succeeded in firing a shot. Its bullet sent Brady's hat spinning from the Kid's head. Then the Mexican followed his companions as Texan lead caused them to crash to the ground.

Coming out of the darkness with their rifles held ready for further use, Brady Anchor and Jefferson Trade converged on the Kid. Although four of the Mexicans' horses had fled, the other three had been brought down by their hobbles as they had attempted to do so. However, the Kid's well-trained Appaloosa was standing at the edge of the clearing where it had come to a halt after obeying his signal to walk away.

"*Gracias amigos,*" the Kid drawled, moving forward with the intention of ensuring that none of the gang could resume hostilities.

"*Es nada,*" Jefferson Trade answered, advancing to help with the examination. At its conclusion, he looked to where his uncle was attending to the three hobbled horses. "They're all cashed in."

"I'll not do much mourning for them," Brady replied. "Happen you don't have any notions contrary-wise, Kid, we'll deliver 'em to the sheriff at Eagle Pass."

"It'd be's well to," the Kid conceded. "I'm right obliged to you for helping."

"You don't need to be," Brady answered, as he and the two young men walked from the clearing. "We saw what they did to a rancher and his family over to Val Verde County just afore Christmas. Which's one reason we brought word that they were gunning for you."

"Figured's how odds of seven to two was just a lil mite higher than we could handle," Jefferson continued frankly, "and's how you'd likely be willing to help us whittle 'em down a mite. Only we never thought you'd want to do it the way you did."

"I allowed it was the only way, 'cept for bushwacking 'em and I didn't reckon you'd've stood for that," the Kid replied. "In spite of what I told the folks back there, I knew that Es-cuchador'd try to kill me no matter how much explaining I did. At least, doing it my way gave him the chance to change his mind."

"There's one thing puzzling me, though," Brady remarked. "Likely it's none of my never-mind, but—knowing who and *what* she is—why did Rosa Rio pass word to the marshal that Escuchador was gunning for you?"

"Maybe she's got religion and did it out of the good of her heart," the Kid suggested mildly.

"It *could've* happened that way, just like I *could've* voted Republican," Brady admitted. "Only I'd be inclined to think there was a mite more to it than that."

"Fact being," Jefferson went on, "if we didn't know it wasn't likely, Uncle Brady 'n' me'd've thought she was scared you'd reckon she sent him after you and wanted to make sure you knew it wasn't so. Only Rosa Rio wouldn't be scared—would she?"

"Like I said, Kid," Brady continued. "Maybe it's none of our never-mind and we hope you'll forgive us for acting nosey. But, not that we'd like too many folks to get to know about it, we're Texas Rangers and it makes us act that way when there's something's we don't understand."

"Happen you can wait until we get back to the camp, seeing's how the folks're to have heard the shooting and'll be worrying," the Kid drawled. "I'll tell you when we get there."

"Well, by gad!" Guillemot boomed, slapping a fat thigh appreciatively as the Kid completed the story of his visit to Rosa Rio's *cantina.* "If that doesn't beat anything I've ever heard! You *are* a remarkable young man, Mr. Ysabel. Wouldn't you say so, Mr. Anchor?"

"I reckon you don't know just how remarkable," Brady Anchor replied, being able to imagine what such a visit must have entailed.

Sitting on her opened-out bed roll, Belle Boyd had been watching Guillemot's and Silk's reactions as they had listened to the Kid. She had noticed that the secretary's face had grown more surly as his employer had shown interest and approbation.

The Rebel Spy had not been particularly surprised to discover that Belle Starr had contrived to eavesdrop on her conversation with Silk, although she had appreciated the other girl's skill in having passed through the bushes so silently that her presence had not been detected. However, they had not been able to debate the matter upon which the lady outlaw had commented due to Boyd being in a position where Guillemot could have seen her. So Boyd had descended the slope to join him and Starr had gone back to her position.

Boyd had been relieved when the Kid, Brady Anchor, Jefferson Trade and Salt-Hoss had arrived unharmed. While Guillemot and Starr had shared the Rebel Spy's sentiments, Silk had barely been able to hide his disappointment over the young Texan's safe return. Having insisted on hearing what had happened, the Ox had clearly been impressed by the way in which the Kid handled the situation and was even more so on learning why Rosa Rio had been so obliging as to send the warning.

"There's some riders coming," Jefferson Trade remarked, standing up with his rifle in his hand.

"Five or six of them" the Kid supplemented. "They're not trying to sneak up on us, noise they're making, but you ladies'd maybe best move back out of the firelight until we know for sure who they are."

Although the girls obeyed, the precaution proved to be unnecessary. Even before they appeared on the southern side of the valley, the riders had announced themselves as being the sheriff of Maverick County and his posse.

"You folks wouldn't happen to've seen or heard a rider in the past hour or so, would you?" the peace officer inquired, after he and his men had dismounted in response to Guillemot's invitation.

"No," the Ox replied. "Who are you after?"

"A *pistolero* called Matt Urizza," the sheriff answered. "He walked into the Eagle Pass Hotel and threw down on a couple of dudes who were having a meal. Killed 'em both, but got hit in the shoulder afore they went down. He still managed to light out, though, and we're after him."

"Dudes, you say," Guillemot remarked. "Do you know why he did it?"

"Nope," the sheriff admitted and eyed the fat man in a speculative manner as he gave further information. "Seems like Urizza walked in, they saw him, started to get up and he threw down on 'em. No offence meant, but you wouldn't know 'em by any chance?"

"I'm afraid I can't help you," the Ox lied, after the sheriff had described the victims in a way which suggested that they were the Germans, Ehlring and Werra. Then he indicated Belle Boyd who had returned from the darkness along with Belle Starr. "This is General Hardin's granddaughter, she is acting as my hostess on a hunting trip."

"I didn't reckon I'd be lucky enough to meet somebody who knew the dudes," the sheriff drawled, when Guillemot had introduced the rest of his party. "What brought us out this way was we heard shooting a while back and concluded we'd best find out what it was all about."

"We had a run in with Juan Escuchador and his bunch," the Kid explained.

"Looks like you come off easy," the sheriff declared, glancing around. "Which way'd they go when they lit out?"

"They didn't exactly light out, 'cept one," the Kid replied and explained why the gang had failed to do so.

"Can't say's I blame you for handling it like you did," the sheriff stated at the end of the story. "They'd've gunned all of you given a chance."

"We couldn't fetch the bodies in with us," the Kid went on. "All their hosses either ran off or got hurt through being throwed by their hobbles, so we came back to borrow some of Mr. Guillemot's."

"We'll go and fetch 'em for you," the sheriff offered. "And if you'll let me use some of your stock, I'll send 'em back to you, sir."

"You can use them and welcome," Guillemot answered. "But you don't need to send them back, we'll collect them on our way through Eagle Pass."

Accepting Brady Anchor's suggestion that he and his nephew would guide the posse to the bodies, the sheriff had set off with them after having some coffee.

On returning to the fire, after having helped the sheriff select three horses to be used for transporting the bodies to Eagle Pass, the Kid sensed there was trouble in the air.

Looking angry, Belle Starr was confronting Silk. Belle Boyd was standing near Guillemot, who sat studying the lady outlaw in an appraising manner. However, Silk swung his attention from Starr. Looking at the Kid, he raised his left hand towards the lapel of his jacket. Taking a warning from the hint of malicious satisfaction on the secretary's face, the Kid came to a halt by the back of the buckboard. In a casual-seeming fashion, he dropped his right hand on to the Winchester which he had placed there when satisfied that the posse were who they had claimed to be.

"You look like a man with something on his mind," the Kid remarked, adopting a provocative attitude.

"I'm wondering how the Germans knew enough to be waiting for us at Eagle Pass," Silk answered. "As Miss Beauregard pointed out, *she* didn't know where we were going. And only one other person here saw, or spoke to, them."

"That'd be *me*, I reckon," the Kid said quietly.

"It would," Silk agreed.

"And *you* figure's I told them?" the Kid asked, just as gently.

"You're the only one who spoke to them—!" Silk began, hoping that he could provoke the young Texan into a hostile move which would justify him in drawing.

The hope materialized, but not as the secretary would have wished.

Given no hint of his intentions, the Kid scooped up his Winchester. Although he did not point the barrel in Silk's direction, his left hand closed on the foregrip and his right forefinger was inside the triggerguard.

Taken by surprise, as the Kid made the very rapid and unexpected transition from apparent unpreparedness to complete readiness, Silk allowed the comment to die away unfinished. He was painfully aware that the Indian-dark Texan held a weapon which was far more readily available for use than was his own holstered revolver.

"Go on," the Kid challenged and his face had the cold, hard, menacing savagery of a *Pehnane* Dog Soldier. "*Spit* her out, *hombre*."

"*Ysabel!*" Boyd shouted, stepping forward; but, as Starr noticed, halting before she had come between the two men. "How *dare* you threaten Mr. Silk?"

"I wouldn't say I'm threatening anybody," the Kid contradicted. "All I'm doing is making sure I'll get a chance to say my piece. That *hombre's* too jumpy and handy with a gun for me to want him suspicioning me of having sold out to the Germans."

"I don't think that Silk meant it quite like that, Mr. Ysabel," Guillemot put in soothingly. "And Miss Beauregard gave us a perfectly satisfactory answer to how they knew where we'd be crossing the river."

"That's right," Starr agreed, glaring indignantly at the secretary. "They'd guess that Mr. Guillemot wouldn't be riding a horse and Eagle Pass's the nearest place to San Antonio that we could take the rig across."

"And I'm inclined to believe that is what happened," Guillemot declared. "So I'd be obliged if you would let the whole matter drop, Silk."

Turning away angrily, the secretary faced Belle Boyd. The look which she gave him said as plainly as any words, "I told you he was on Ysabel's side against you."

CHAPTER THIRTEEN

The Knife Is Yours, *Cabrito*

"Tomorrow I will show you some really exciting sport, gentlemen," Don Arsenio Serrano promised his guests after they had finished their dinner on the night of their arrival, and he waved a hand towards the weapon which his senior servant had placed on the table. "And then we will talk further about the knife."

The remainder of the journey to *Casa* Serrano had been almost without incident. Although Anthony Silk had clearly been displeased and embittered over Octavius Xavier Guillemot's acceptance of Belle Starr's theory regarding the Germans, he had kept his objections to himself. Moving on the following morning, the party had collected the horses which had been loaned to the sheriff at Eagle Pass and had heard that Matteo Urizza had been shot by a rancher while attempting to steal a fresh mount.

Crossing the Rio Grande on the ferry which operated between Eagle Pass and the Mexican town of Pierdras Negras, the party had followed the route which had been suggested by the Ysabel Kid. Wanting to avoid attracting unwanted attention, which might have brought *bandidos* down upon them, the Kid had insisted that they did not stay on the trail that would have taken them through Zaragoza. He had had another, unmentioned, reason for going across country.

There had been no further confrontations between the Kid and Silk, only a smouldering, thinly-veiled hostility which had threatened to erupt without actually having done so. Belle Boyd had been responsible for that, having warned Silk that they could not hope to reach their destination without the Kid's aid. Becoming aware of the difficulties once they had left the trail, Silk had appreciated the girl's point of view and had held his temper in check. For his part, realizing that an extra gun might make the difference between life and death if they should be attacked by *bandidos* or Yaqui Indians, the Kid had been content to allow the peaceful conditions to continue. However, his every instinct had warned him that Silk intended to force a showdown eventually.

While the Rebel Spy had been successful in keeping the peace, she had been less fortunate in another matter where Silk was concerned. As they could not find an opportunity to be alone, she had been unable to resume the conversation which had been interrupted by the shooting on the night that the Kid had dealt with Juan Escuchador.

On reaching the *Rio de la Babia,* the party had made the crossing by floating the buckboard over supported by logs. They had then spent the night in a deserted adobe house near to the edge of a very deep and narrow chasm through which the river poured in raging, churning rapids. Going upstream for a couple of miles, they had turned along the *Rio Ventoso* and had followed it to their destination.

Despite their unexpected arrival, the party had been made welcome by Don Arsenio Serrano. He had grown into a silver-haired, distinguished-looking man with the courtly manners of a Spanish *grandee*. Apologizing for his inability to speak English, he had suggested that they might like to refresh themselves before dinner. So they had been assigned to rooms in his magnificent, well-protected house. After the girls—each of whom had brought a stylish dress and jewelry in her baggage—the Kid, Guillemot and Silk had bathed and changed into clean clothing, they had joined their host in the dining-room. The secretary was at a disadvantage, as he alone could not speak Spanish. At Salt-Hoss's own request, he had been accommodated with and was being entertained by the *vaqueros*. They were, as the old timer had pointed out, his kind of people.

Learning of the reason for the visit, Serrano had hidden the surprise which he must have felt. He had remarked, somewhat wryly, that he would not have thought anybody had read his uncle's history of the family. Beyond Guillemot admitting that the book had been his source of information, the comment had gone unexplained. However, Serrano had shown no hesitation about ordering his *majordomo* to fetch the knife from his study.

"May I look at it, Don Arsenio?" Guillemot requested, accepting his host's promise to consider the matter of its return to the Bowie family without question.

"Of course," Serrano agreed, drawing off the sheath and holding out the knife.

Watching Guillemot turning the great knife over and over, the Kid was impressed by his self control. While the young Texan—and, probably, the girls and Silk—could sense his great excitement, nothing of it showed on his now sun-reddened and bland features. To all appearances, the Ox might have been examining something in which he had only a marginal interest rather than the goal of a long and costly quest.

"With all respect, *Senor* Guillemot," Serrano remarked, watching the fat man holding and studying the hilt of the knife, "I wish that my hands were as large as yours. I can't hold the handle comfortably, nor can any of my men."

"Couldn't you have had it cut down to size, Don Arsenio?" Belle Boyd inquired and noticed that Guillemot stiffened slightly.

"I thought of having it done when I came home," Serrano admitted. "But our blacksmith, who was very good at his work, warned me that to do so would ruin the knife's balance. As I didn't wish for that to happen, I kept it untouched as a memento of a not unimportant period of my life."

"Did your blacksmith dismantle it to make his examination?" Gullemot inquired and it was obvious to the other members of his party, if not to their host, that he found the possibility disturbing.

"No," Serrano replied. "He just looked and felt at it. Then he said it was the finest weapon he had ever seen, which was no mean compliment, and warned me that any alteration would spoil it. So I left it as it was. To be quite honest, it was far too big and heavy for my taste."

"I can see that you would like to look at it, Mr. Ysabel," Guillemot commented, acting more relaxed now that he had received a negative answer to his question and offering the weapon to the young Texan.

"Whee-dogie!" the Kid ejaculated in English, as he took the massive and gleaming knife. He found it to be somewhat heavier and, with its enlarged handle, not so well balanced in his grasp as his own product of James Black's forge. "Old Jim Bowie must've had a real big fist—" Then, remembering where he was, reverted to Spanish and continued politely, "My apologies, Don Arsenio, but I never thought that I'd be holding Colonel Bowie's own blade. I've heard about it all my life. Is it true that it can cut through an ordinary knife?"

"It can," Serrano answered, smiling at the normally impassive young Texan's enthusiasm. He picked up one of the table-knives and went on, "I have heard of your ability as a knife-fighter, *Cabrito*. Would you care to try?"

"How about you doing it, Mr. Guillemot?" the Kid suggested, holding out Bowie's knife. "You can use it one-handed."

Watched by the men and girls, Guillemot grasped the big weapon's hilt in his right hand. Accepting the table-knife with his left, he held it with the end of the cutting edge resting on the table. Tentatively at first, he brought the blade of the bowie knife into contact. Then, making a sawing motion, he caused it to sever the other knife without any great difficulty.

"Whee-dogie!" the Kid breathed, the comment brought from him before he could prevent it. Not that he needed to be concerned over his display of emotion. The rest of the party were duplicating it in their own individual fashions.

"You might not believe me," Serrano remarked, clearly enjoying the response created by the experiment and watching Guillemot examining the bowie knife's cutting edge, "But I have never done more than rub up the edge on a razor-strop a couple of times a year and yet it stays as sharp as ever."

"I'm most impressed, sir," Guillemot declared, returning

the knife to its owner. He intended to go on with a comment about the impossibility of duplicating the steel due to it having been created from a solitary fragment from a "star."

"So were Pascual and the other leaders of the Ventoso Yaquis when they saw me cut one of their lances' head in two," Serrano replied, before the Ox could continue, sliding the knife into its sheath.

"Do you get much trouble with the Yaquis, *senor?*" the Kid inquired, knowing that the tribe in question were to Mexico what the Comanches had been to Texas and the Apaches still were to New Mexico or Arizona.

"None," Serrano replied. "At least, not since I armed all my *vaqueros* with Winchester repeaters. After one attack, which cost them many lives, the chiefs agreed to talk peace. Now we trade together and some of their people even work on the *hacienda*. Of course, to save the chiefs' faces if some hot-headed young brave wants to attack us, I pay them a small tribute of horses, mules and cattle twice a year."

"You say that they've seen you cut through the head of a lance, senor?" the Kid asked.

"That was during the first meeting," Serrano answered. "Since then, I've repeated the trick at each visit. It amuses them."

"Have any of them ever tried it?" the Kid wanted to know.

"Several have, over the years," Serrano admitted off-hand-edly, clearly attaching no importance to the matter. "However, the Yaqui tend to be of middle height and stocky and only one of them has been able to use the knife one-handed. A young brave called *Manos Grande* can do so."

"Big Hand," the Kid translated, half to himself, then ad-dressed his host. "You say *he* can do it, *senor?*"

"He cut through a knife with it during the Christmas visit," Serrano confirmed. "His companions were highly delighted to see him do it."

"Yes, sir," the Kid said soberly. "I can see how they might be."

"What kind of sport are we to have tomorrow, Don Ar-senio?" Guillemot put in, wanting to change the subject before the Kid reminded Serrano any further about the knife's value.

"It is something that a cousin from Spain who had been to

India taught to us when he paid me a visit," Serrano explained. "The *vaqueros* enjoy it very much. It is called 'pig-sticking.'"

"There one goes!" Serrano yelled excitedly, reining his big white gelding to a halt and pointing to where a swiftly-moving brown animal burst from a clump of bushes ahead of the line of *peons,* who were acting as beaters, and fled at considerable speed across the rolling terrain. "After it!"

Elaborating on his answer to Guillemot's question the previous evening, Serrano had told his guests how a number of pigs had escaped during a Yaqui attack in the early 1830's. Many of the animals had never been recovered and, finding conditions on the range to their liking, had gone feral. Subsequent generations had gradually reverted to the physical appearance and behavior patterns of wild swine, increasing in numbers until they had become the cause of considerable damage. However, the visit by a cousin from Spain had shown a way in which the animals could not only be controlled, but would also provide an exciting kind of sport which the *vaqueros,* natural-born horsemen, had found very much to their liking.

Serrano had said that the hunt would be conducted in a similar manner to that developed by the British "tent clubs" in India. However, there was one variation. Hunting over fairly open country, the Mexicans had found that lances of between eight foot six inches and nine foot in length were more suitable than the six foot six inches variety used by the British.[1] The participants would be formed into three-man "heats," taking turns to pursue the pigs once they had been flushed by the beaters.

On being asked if he would care to take part in the hunt, Guillemot had pointed out that his bulk precluded him from horseback riding. So Serrano had offered to put a buggy at his disposal and he could follow in it. Although both of the girls had proclaimed willingness to participate, they had been told that doing so would be too dangerous and they were to be restricted to the role of spectators. That had left the Kid and

1. With the exception of the Calcutta Tent Club, the British eventually adopted a longer type of spear.

Silk to uphold the honor of the visitors. With his Comanche upbringing and Dog Soldier's regard for a lance as a weapon—he had been initiated into full membership of the supreme *Pehnane* war lodge as a boy—and despite the years he had lived among white people, the Kid had been delighted by the opportunity to do so. Silk had clearly been less enamored by the prospect, but could hardly have refused when Serrano had suggested that he acted as representative for his employer.

Soon after dawn, the party had assembled. While they were eating breakfast, Serrano had told the Kid and Silk that they would be members of his heat. He had also placed horses which had been trained for, and gained experience in, the business of pig-sticking at their disposal. From all appearances, he had gauged his guests' potential as riders with some accuracy. He had assigned a steady-looking brown gelding to Silk. The Kid had been supplied with a smallish, ugly *bayo-cebrunos*[2] stallion. Studying it, he had decided that it possessed the indefinable quality known as *brio escondido*,[3] and would be a most reliable mount for what he suspected would be tricky and dangerous work. Watched by the grinning and appreciative *vaqueros*, he had quickly asserted his dominance over the horse. By the time they had reached the area over which they would be hunting, he was in full control and had known that he was sitting an animal upon which he could place complete dependence.

Being guests of Serrano, it had been accepted that the Kid and Silk should have the opportunity to chase the first pig. So, having delivered his command, the *haciendero* set his mount into motion.

"Hee-yah!" whooped the Kid, feeling the little stallion quivering with readiness beneath him and allowing it to spring forward.

With the young Texan to his left and Silk to his right, fanning out so they had room to maneuver, Serrano led the way through the line of beaters. For all his years, he set a hard pace across the anything but smooth and even country.

Keeping the *bayo-cebrunos* under control, the Kid once again tested the weight and balance of the lance in his right

2. *Bayo-cebrunos:* a dun shading into a smokey-grey color.
3. *Brio escondido:* "hidden vigor," stamina and endurance of a high quality.

hand. Nine foot in length, with a needle-pointed and diamond-shaped head counter-balanced by a lead-loaded butt, it compared favorably with the type of Comanche weapon which he had handled as a boy and since. So he was eager to test it in the sport of pig-sticking. His every instinct gave warning that such a pastime would call for riding skill of a very high order and, even to a person who possessed the requisite ability, it might become a dangerous and exciting occupation.

For all his eagerness, the Kid did not forget the rules which Serrano had explained as they were riding to the hunting area. Once the prey had been flushed by the beaters, the members of the heat had to decide whether or not it was "rideable." As neither he nor Silk could claim sufficient knowledge to make such a decision, they had agreed that it should be their host's prerogative. What was more, they had suggested that Serrano should take the center position and demonstrate how the sticking was carried out. Of course, as he told them, if the designated animal should "jink," or swerve aside, the rider in front of whom it was moving would be permitted to deal with it—or to try to.

Watching Serrano, Silk was hoping that he would hold out his lance horizontally at arm's length to signal that the pig was unworthy and would not be "rideable."

The hope did not materialize.

"On! On! On!" Serrano yelled, lowering his spear's tip to the vertical and giving the traditional order for the pursuit to continue.

"He's rideable!'" the Kid yelled, excitement causing him to forget his dislike of the secretary and to explain their host's decision.

Having passed on the order, the Kid turned his full attention to the fleeing animal. Although originally descended from domestic stock, the big boar neither looked nor acted like its ancestors. About thirty-four inches in height at the shoulder, it weighed close to two hundred and sixty pounds; which did not make it slow or clumsy. Just the opposite in fact. Short-backed, tapering to the hips from a long-snouted head that was armed with a pair of curved and very sharp tushes, it was a solid mass of steel-hard muscles which propelled it across the range at a very high speed. Its wild nature and agility showed in the way that it selected the roughest ground over which to flee.

Half a mile of fast and furious galloping was needed before the heat began to close with their quarry. However, by that time Silk had fallen well behind the other two. Being unwilling to accept the risks involved in such a reckless chase, he restrained his mount's eagerness and held it forcibly to a much safer pace than that of his companions.

Although the Kid could tell that he had the swifter horse, he refrained from forging ahead of his host. Not only did he have the rules to consider, but he had talked with the *vaqueros* on the journey to the hunting area. They had told him about the sounder of pigs which they were expecting to find. Its leader, the big boar which Serrano and he were now pursuing, had evaded several previous attempts to ride it down. As the *vaqueros* had mentioned that their *patron* had set his heart on doing so, the Kid considered that it would be impolite to circumvent him. Only if the animal jinked to the left, or something untoward happened, could the young Texan intervene.

"He's tiring, *Cabrito!*" Serrano called, flickering a brief glance to his left as the boar sped towards a small clump of bushes. He did not look to the right as he had already discovered that Silk had fallen behind. "It won't be long before—"

Instead of going into the bushes, the boar swerved around them. However, as it went by, a second pig erupted from beneath them and dashed, squealing in alarm, in front of Serrano. Startled by the pig, the white gelding swung violently to the right. Taken by surprise, the elderly Mexican was thrown from his saddle. Letting the lance fall, he crashed into the top of the bushes and went onwards over them. While they lessened the force of his fall, he was winded by his impact with the ground.

At that moment, having grown tired of fleeing, the big boar seemed to reverse direction in its own length. Letting out an awesome snorting screech, it charged towards the dazed and helpless man.

Dropping the head of his lance, the Kid was on the point of trying to take the second pig when he saw Serrano thrown and the boar swirling around to return. So, realizing that his host was in terrible peril, he forgot the smaller pig. Guiding the *bayo-cebrunos* in the required direction, he let out a *Pehn-ane* war yell and kicked its ribs. Although already galloping at a good speed, the little horse increased its pace as it hurled at a tangent towards the boar.

Seeing its new assailant, the boar swung to meet the challenge. Relying upon his mount, the Kid concentrated his attention towards the bristling beast which was rushing in his direction. Holding the lance in an underhand grip, he aimed the point as he had been taught by his maternal grandfather.

From the way in which the two animals were converging, it seemed that they would collide and the horse be ripped open by the boar's great tushes. Knowing its work, the little stallion swerved at the last moment and just sufficiently to avoid being disembowelled. Hearing the fearsome chomping as the boar's jaws opened and closed, the Kid thrust with the lance. Its diamond-shaped head passed betwen the boar's ears to sink home just behind the shoulders. Such was the impetus that it impaled the powerful body. Allowing the lance to slip from his grasp as he was carried by the stricken animal, he concentrated both hands on the work of turning his speeding mount. Responsive to the instructions which it was receiving, the stallion went into a rump-scraping turn. Transferring his right hand from the reins to the butt of the old Dragoon Colt, the Kid was ready to draw and fire. The need to do so did not arise, for the boar was sprawled lifeless on its side some feet from where Serrano was lying.

Riding towards his host, the Kid saw the other members of the party approaching. Silk was nearest, pushing his horse faster than he had done during the chase. The rest were coming as swiftly as they could, with Belle Boyd and Belle Starr among the leaders. Showing considerable driving skill, Guillemot was bringing up the rear at a good speed. Bringing the stallion to a halt, the Kid dropped from his saddle. To his relief, he saw that Serrano was staring at the boar and trying to rise.

"Are you hurt, *senor?*" the Kid inquired, helping the Mexican to his feet.

"Only my pride," Serrano confessed with a wry smile. "I think I'm getting too old for this kind of sport."

"I wouldn't say that, *senor,*" the Kid said with a grin, glancing to where Silk was dismounting from the brown geld-

ing. "You were unlucky, nothing more. I apologize for taking
what should have been your kill."

"If you hadn't—" Serrano began, nodding towards the impaled carcass of the boar. "You saved my life, *Cabrito.*"

"You'd have done the same for me, *senor,*" the Kid pointed
out.

"Perhaps," Serrano smiled. "Anyway, the knife is yours,
Cabrito."

"What?" the Kid gasped.

"I have no son or grandson to whom I can leave it when
I die," Serrano explained. "So I give it to you. Do what you
will with it."

CHAPTER FOURTEEN

A Whole *Hill* Of Such Steel

"Well, sir," Octavius Xavier Guillemot said, as he sat on the chair which had been offered to him and wasting no time in getting down to the business that had brought him to the Ysabel Kid's room after the rest of the household had retired for the night. "I hope that you will not think it forward of me if I suggest that you ignore Miss Hardin's uncalled-for and unjustifiable ultimatum."

"How do you mean?" the Kid inquired, glancing to where James Bowie's knife lay on the dressing-table.

Although Don Arsenio Serrano's gift had placed the weapon in the Kid's possession, he still did not know why the Ox was attaching so much importance to it. So he and Belle Boyd had staged a little scene which they had hoped would produce the required information. On their return from the hunt, she had waited until only Guillemot was close enough to hear and had stated that the Kid must turn the knife over to her "grandfather." On the Kid pointing out that it had been presented to him by their host, she had warned that unless he acceded to her demand General Hardin would fire him and make sure that nobody in Texas would give him employment. Then, apparently becoming aware of the Ox's presence, she had stalked away.

"If you will accept the advice of an older, more experienced man," Guillemot replied, "you will not hand the knife over to her grandfather."

"Well, I don't know about that," the Kid said soberly. "It's not a whole heap of use to me, seeing that I can't use it and to have it cut down to my fit'd spoil it. On top of that, Ole Devil could make things mighty bad for me happen I crossed him."

"You mean that he would discharge you?"

"Likely. And there's not many in Texas's'd dare go against him if he passed the word I wasn't to be taken on. So I might's well let him have it. Likely he'll give me a couple of hundred dollars for it."

"If that's all he gives you, you will be cheated," Guillemot stated. "The knife is worth much, *much* more than a paltry few hundred dollars in the right circles."

"I'm listening," the Kid drawled.

"Come, sir," the Ox boomed. "You are an intelligent young man. Surely you don't believe that I have travelled from Europe merely to collect and return the knife to the Bowie family?"

"I'd sorta got a notion you could have something else in mind," the Kid admitted. "And I'd a sneaking feeling that Jim Bowie's blade must be worth plenty of money, there being so many fellers trying to take it from you. So, afore we do any hoss-trading, I'd like to know a lil mite more about the stock."

"I'll do better that that, sir," Guillemot promised. "I'll tell you the full story. Then you will be able to judge for yourself how valuable the knife is."

"That's right obliging of you, sir," the Kid declared and sat on the bed with an air of expectancy.

"I suppose you know the story of how the knife was made?" Guillemot began.

"Well, I've allus heard's how it was made from a piece of a star that James Black found near his forge in Arkansas," the Kid answered. "Which can't be why it's so valuable, as the only way you could make steel like it was if you'd more lumps from the same star."

"The story is true, sir," Guillemot insisted, neither confirming nor arguing against the young Texan's comment. "But only up to a point. While the knife was manufactured from a fragment of what you refer to as a 'star,' it came into Black's possession in a somewhat different manner. The ore came into his hands when a badly injured man arrived at his forge. Despite all Black could do for him, the man died. However, before he did, he gave Black several pieces of metal and told him where they had come from. Apparently he was an English geologist who had been on an expedition in Texas and had made a find of such magnitude that he had been coming to visit Black with the hope that they could exploit his discovery, but was waylaid by thieves and shot as he had escaped. After he died, Black examined the pieces and realized that he had come into possession of something unique. They were lumps of raw ore, sir, but of steel and of such a quality that it was far in advance of anything which could be produced in the 1830s—or today for that matter—"

"That'd be right useful, happen there was more of it," the Kid commented.

"There is, sir, there is!" Guillemot stated and the excitement in his voice was far from being assumed. "A hill which, under the soil, is a solid piece of it. Can you imagine that, sir, a whole *hill* of such steel?"

"How'd it get there?"

"Possibly as Black said, by falling from the sky. Such things have been known to have happened, sir, but on a smaller scale. To go on, though, Black had the information to guide him to the hill, but he lacked the means to do so. Then fate brought a solution. James Bowie arrived at Black's forge, bringing a wooden model from which he wanted a knife to be created. One with special features and made to fit his massive hand. As you no doubt know, sir, in addition to being a knife-fighter par excellence and an adventurer, Bowie was also a shrewd businessman. Black took him into his confidence and they became partners. However, each of them realized that to exploit the hill to its full advantage would require far more capital than

they could put out. They also knew that they would have to
have some more concrete evidence before any businessman
would condescend to back them. So Black carved the directions
which he had been given into the handle of the knife which he
was making from the largest piece of the 'star.' With the ivory
grips in place, the carving could not be seen. Nor would their
presence be suspected. I believe that the idea may have come
from Bowie. While nobody would think twice about a man
with his reputation carrying the knife, they might have grown
suspicious if he was seen examining a sheet of paper. Or it
could have been lost, or destroyed, with far more ease than
the knife could. Anyway, Bowie went to Texas and found the
hill—"

"I've never heard tell of it happening," the Kid objected.

"He did not speak of his find, naturally, sir," Guillemot
replied. "Not even to his brother and the other men who had
accompanied him. They suspected that, while he was off on
his own, he had discovered a lost Spanish mine and never
imagined that the actual find was something infintely more
valuable. Knowing the nature of the Mexican authorities,
Bowie was aware that one hint of the truth would cause himself
and Black to be deprived of any benefits which they might
otherwise have hoped to acrue. That was one of the reasons
why they decided to seek financial support in Europe rather
than from the United States."

"Seeing's how nobody's ever started to dig up the hill and
make this kind of steel," the Kid drawled and indicated the
knife, "I'd say they didn't get it."

"That's true," the Ox conceded.

"Folks in Europe wouldn't believe them, huh?" the Kid
asked.

"They believed Black, who came over, to a certain degree,"
Guillemot corrected. "I tell you, sir, his arrival created a sensation in England, Germany and France. In addition to having
brought pieces of the ore, he had four clasp-knives which he
had made from it. Two were from the raw ore and the others
blended with it and the best steel he could manufacture. Even
the latter were vastly superior to any steel Europe had ever
seen. This is one of them." Reaching into the pocket of his
smoking jacket, he produced the knife and offered it to the

young Texan, continuing, "It came into my possession when I was commissioned to obtain either the location of the hill, or to discover Black's system of smelting and producing the steel if he should be doing so by other means. I must confess that, due to the bungling of an assistant, I failed in my mission. While she learned the story which I have just told you, her informant did not supply her with the knowledge that was required."

"Then you still don't know whether there is a hill, or if James Black was making it?"

"He wasn't making it. That was the respective, but unanimous decision of experts from the major steel manufacturing companies of Great Britain, Germany and France. However, all of them told him basically the same thing. While interested in his proposition, none was willing to incur the heavy expenses of mining the ore and working it with conditions so unstable in Mexican-controlled Texas. Although disappointed, Black did not despair, for he knew that the Americans in Texas were already commencing their struggle to establish independence from Mexican rule. So he returned home to await developments. When they came, they were not of a satisfactory nature. Bowie was killed at the Alamo and a few weeks later Black died in a hunting accident. Neither of them left any written record of their arrangement, nor of the hill's location.

"I must confess that my interest in the affair waned when I heard of this. The only means by which the hill could be discovered, without a *very* long search, would have been to obtain Bowie's knife, which I assumed, correctly, had been carried off by one of the Mexicans who had been responsible for his death. I tried to discover who it might be and failed."

"That's not what *I'd* say, seeing's we're sat talking here like this," the Kid objected. "It looks to a half-smart lil Texas boy like me's you must have found out."

"I did, sir," Guillemot admitted. "But not for a number of years. In fact, it was only last year that a brilliant young acquaintance of mine, Professor James Moriarty, rearoused my interest. A remarkable young man, James, I'm sure that he will go far in our way of business.[1] Anyway, he was hired as tutor

---

1. According to Sir Arthur Conan Doyle's Sherlock Holmes stories, Professor James Moriarty justified Guillemot's faith in his abilities.

for the youngest son of a Squire Holmes in Yorkshire. Apparently James and the son took an instant dislike to each other, but James stayed in his father's employment for a time. Holmes had travelled extensively on the Continent and had a sizeable library to which James had access. More to test his knowledge of Spanish than for any other reason, he started to read *A History of the Serrano Family,* by Eugenio, Duke of Zamora. In it, James read of how our host had served in the North Coahuila Militia under Santa Anna at the Siege of the Alamo. He had been responsible for the death of James Bowie and had carried off his famous knife as a trophy of war, taking care that nobody knew so that his superiors could not take it from him. Fleeing from the Battle of San Jacinto, he was waylaid by Texian ruffians and his life was saved by *'Diablo Viejo,'* Old Devil Hardin, to whom he expressed gratitude. I saw in this last piece a way in which I might gain possession of the knife. Coming to the United States, I located Resin Bowie the Second and won his confidence by pretending to wish to write a history of his family. I also told him of my discovery and suggested that I should visit Serrano with the dual objective of learning how James came to die and, if possible, to secure the return of his knife to his kin-folk—"

"Without mentioning about the hill of steel," the Kid guessed with a grin.

"As he clearly knew nothing about it, I saw no reason to say anything which might cause him to doubt my motives," the Ox replied, also smiling. "At my instigation, he wrote to General Hardin and you know the rest."

"Huh huh," the Kid grunted as the Ox sat back and looked at him expectantly.

"I have, of course, more in mind than just satisfying your curiosity," Guillemot warned.

"I sort of figured you might have," the Kid admitted.

"Having come so far and expended a not inconsiderable amount of money on the quest for Bowie's blade," the Ox went on, "I was naturally perturbed to learn that Serrano had given the knife to you. But then I told myself, 'Mr. Ysabel is an intelligent young man and will appreciate my being completely frank with him.' So I have been."

"And I'm right obliged to you for doing it."

"May I ask, in the light of what you now know, what you intend to do with the knife, sir?"

"One thing's for sure," the Kid stated firmly. "I'm not going to hand it over to General Hardin."

"How will you dispose of it?" Guillemot inquired.

"Sell it, I reckon."

"To whom?"

"There seemed to be plenty of folks after it," the Kid began hesitantly.

"And they are all dead," the Ox reminded him. "No, sir, *you* can't dispose of it." He raised a fat hand to silence the young Texan's protest before it could be uttered. "Capable as you are in many ways, sir, handling the financial ramifications of a matter like this would leave you as lost as I would be alone on the range."

"You could be right at that," the Kid conceded.

"Then, sir, as your ownership of the knife was in part at least brought about through my efforts, and as I am eminently qualified to make the most advantageous negotiations, I wonder if you would consider a partnership?"

"That'd depend on how we'd cut the pot," the Kid said cagily.

"I have expended a considerable sum already—"

"I'm not gainsaying it."

"And I assure you that no small amount is involved—"

"Would a sixty-forty cut, your way, suit you?" the Kid asked.

"By gad, sir!" Guillemot boomed and extended his right hand. "You have a deal."

Carrying the Winchester rifle with his left hand grasping the lower end of the foregrip so that it was parallel to the floor, and with his saddle supported on his shoulder with the right, the Kid walked into the main room of the adobe house near to the chasm of the *Rio de la Babia*. As the afternoon was fairly well advanced, he and his party had elected to stay there and make the crossing of the river in the morning.

Although the Kid had apparently accepted Guillemot as his

partner, he had contrived to avoid letting him learn the information that was engraved on the handle of the knife. He had achieved this, without arousing the Ox's suspicions as far as he could tell, by pointing out how neither of them possessed the necessary tools or knowledge to remove and replace the ivory grips and conceal the fact that they had done so. Accepting the comment, Guillemot had also agreed that the Kid should retain the knife and they would leave its examination until after they had parted company with the others in Texas.

The Kid had been adamant regarding the matter of ensuring "Betty Hardin's" safe return to Eagle Pass, stating that—while the money which he obtained as his share from the knife's sale would make him independent of Ole Devil's employment—he intended to continue living in the United States and could not hope to do so if he had allowed harm to come to the General's granddaughter. Having stated that he could understand the Kid's point of view and discussed a few other minor details, Guillemot had returned to his own room.

Waiting until he was sure that the rest of the household could be sleeping, the Kid had visited Belle Boyd and had told her what he had found out. The girl had agreed with the arrangements which he had made and had suggested that they should take no action until they were north of the Rio Grande. They had not attempted to examine the handle, for the same reason that he had given to the Ox.

Spending another day at *Casa* Serrano, the party had commenced the return journey. Wanting to avoid arousing Guillemot's suspicions, the Rebel Spy had carried on with her pose of being "Betty Hardin." She had also continued to cultivate Silk, in the hope that she could learn his plans for gaining possession of the knife. As he had clearly regarded her as playing part in whatever scheme he had in mind, she had persuaded him that it would be unwise to implement it until he was certain he could guide them to safety without the Kid's assistance.

For his part, the Kid had discovered that his "partner" apparently was not content to rely solely upon the binding effect of their hand-shake and verbal agreement. Guillemot had asked Belle Starr to become more friendly with the young Texan and, if possible, to ascertain if he had any ideas about reneging on their arrangement. The lady outlaw's attitude had puzzled the Kid. While warning him of what she was supposed to do, she made no attempt to discover what made the knife so valuable. He doubted that she was as disinterested as appeared on the surface, but had not been able to confirm his suspicions. It was, he had realized, possible that she had no desire to do anything to antagonize a man as influential as Guillemot in criminal circles.

Although there had been some tension, with Boyd acting haughty—but avoiding any action which might have resulted in a confrontation between the Kid and Silk—the journey to the *Rio de la Babia* had been comparatively uneventful. Nor did the Kid anticipate any trouble from the secretary until they were much nearer to Piedras Negras. Certainly Silk had not given Belle Boyd any indication that he might be considering putting his plan into operation.

Having helped Salt-Hoss to attend to the horses, the Kid was the last member of the party apart from the old-timer to enter the house. He found that the girls had already gone into the back room which they would be occupying for the night. As usual, Silk had carried Boyd's saddle for her and was evidently in the girls' quarters. Guillemot was kneeling and opening out his bed roll.

Crossing the room to set his saddle on its side in a corner,[2] where there would be no danger of anybody stepping on it, the Kid glanced at Silk who was coming from the girls' room. There was something in the secretary's attitude which warned the young Texan against laying down his rifle as he had intended. Not only did Silk's face show vicious satisfaction, but his left hand was caressing the jacket's lapel in what had become a familiar and *very* significant manner.

Moving slowly, with the Winchester still held at its point of balance in an apparently negligent fashion, the Kid turned until he was facing the secretary.

"All right, half-breed!" Silk said, every word dripping with sadistic pleasure. "I've been waiting for this. Go for your gun!"

"Is this *your* idea, Mr. Guillemot?" the Kid inquired, without taking his eyes from the secretary.

2. No cowhand ever threw down his saddle, or stood it on its skirts.

"No," the Ox replied.

"Are you backing him on it?" the Kid wanted to know.

"It appears to be a matter between the two of you," Guillemot answered evasively, lurching erect much in the manner of a draught-ox coming to its feet. "So I can hardly take either side. You must see that, sir."

"There you are, half-breed," Silk mocked. "It's just between you and me."

"I won't draw against you," the Kid declared, with deceptive mildness which gave no indication of how prepared he was to spring into instant action. "You're too damned fast for that."

Even as he was answering, the Kid noticed that the girls were standing in the doorway of their room. However, neither of them offered to move or speak. He did not allow their presence to distract him, for he knew that do so while dealing with a man as fast and as deadly as the secretary would be fatal. The Kid had little enough chance of survival as it was, without reducing it any further.

"You don't have any choice," Silk warned, enjoying what he took to be the other's fear of him. "I'm going to kill you one way or the other."

That was, the Kid conceded mentally, all too likely under the circumstances. He was aware of his limitations. It took him well over a second to draw and fire the old Colt Dragoon, while Silk could do the same with his short-barrelled Webley in half of that time. So he could not hope to match the secretary's speed.

There was, as the Kid knew all too well, only one second prize in a gun fight—death!

"Like I said, you're way too fast for me to draw down on," the Kid finally answered, moving his right hand away from the Colt's butt and conscious that Silk was watching it. Then, playing for time, he went on, "You'll be next, happen I go down, Mr. Guillemot."

"Why should I be?" the Ox countered, having no intention of being forced into taking a stand. "Silk is my strong right arm and I trust him implicitly."

"Could be you're trusting the wrong feller," the Kid drawled, standing apparently motionless. Silk's mocking eyes had returned to studying his face and he wanted them to remain there. "I've been thinking a fair bit about those two French *hombres*'s we gunned down in San Antonio. We all figured's they jumped us because they thought I knew it was them who'd whomped me on the head and was coming for 'em."

Drawing a malicious and sadistic pleasure from the situation, Silk did not wish to terminate it too quickly. He was supremely confident in his ability and certain that he could allow the young Texan to make the first move, then kill him before he could bring the heavy old revolver from its holster. So he made no attempt to stop the other from talking, although keeping a careful watch on the Indian-dark features for any suggestion of the thoughts that were concealed by their lack of expression.

Behind Silk, the two girls exchanged worried glances. Each of them had her Remington Double Derringer in her jacket's pocket, but neither offered to take out the weapon. The click of its hammer being drawing to full cock would be heard by the secretary and might—almost certainly would—cause him to draw. So they too stood still and awaited developments.

"If they didn't recognize you—" Guillemot began.

"It wasn't *me* they recognized," the Kid interrupted. "It was Silk, which's why he had to side me instead of letting them gun me down. And why he killed the feller after I'd already wounded him, to make sure he couldn't tell what had happened. I'd say it was your 'strong right arm' and not your 'valley''s sold you out to them."

"You're too smart to live, half-breed!" Silk taunted and his right hand flashed across while the left drew open the side of his jacket for it to reach the Webley's butt without impediment.

While speaking, unnoticed by the secretary, the Kid was allowing the muzzle of his Winchester to sink towards the floor. Then he let the weapon slide very slowly through his fingers until its butt was braced against the rear of his forearm. Still drawing Silk's attention on to his face or, by flickering glances making sure that his right hand was not going any closer to the Dragoon's butt, he contrived to grasp the rifle ready to be fired with his left.

As soon as Silk made his move, so did the Kid. Setting his weight upon his slightly separated feet, he bent his knees a little and, inclining his torso to the rear, adopted much the same posture that combat shooting experts of the future would use when completing a "speed rock" draw.[3]

There was, however, one vital difference in the way that the Kid moved. He had no intention of attempting to circumvent Silk's speed by pulling out the Dragoon. Instead, he pivoted the Winchester into alignment with his left hand. Even as the right was reaching for the foregrip, the rifle bellowed. The bullet took the secretary between the eyes and, bursting out of the back of his head, ploughed into the wall not a foot from where Belle Boyd was standing.

It must be confessed that luck played a considerable part in the Kid making such a supremely effective shot. He had hoped to hit Silk somewhere in the body, or at least to distract the secretary for long enough to permit a more careful aim. Instead, he had been fortunate enough to make an instant kill. Hurled backwards, with the Webley R.I.C. falling unfired from his hand, Silk caused the girls to jump to the rear out of his way and measured his length on the floor of their room.

"I told him that he was too fast for me to draw against," the Kid remarked, swinging his gaze towards Guillemot and ignoring the sound of running feet approaching the front door.

"Thank god you're alive, Lon!" Belle Boyd said fervently, walking towards the Kid although Belle Starr did not follow her. Instead, the lady outlaw retreated into their room. "I'd no idea that he was planning anything like this."

"*Lon!*" Guillemot repeated, taking note of the change in the girl's attitude.

Before any more could be said, Salt-Hoss dashed into the room with his Henry rifle held ready for use. Skidding to a halt, he looked at the body and up to where Starr was walking by it with her Winchester carbine in her hands.

"Put your rifle down slow and easy, Kid," the lady outlaw commanded, lining her own weapon at the young Texan. "Then unbuckle your gunbelt and let it fall."

"Do it, *Cuchilo*," Salt-Hoss supplemented, also elevating his Henry into alignment. "We figure what we'll make on selling old Jim Bowie's knife'll set me up in a comfortable ree-tired-ment."

3. A detailed description of the "speed rock" draw is given in: *The ¼-Second Draw.*

CHAPTER FIFTEEN

If Lon Doesn't Get You, I Will

"What do you think you're doing, Miss Beauregard?" Octavius Xavier Guillemot demanded, his florid face darkening with anger as he started to step towards the lady outlaw.

"Stand still!" Belle Starr commanded and her Winchester carbine turned towards the fat man's chest as if it had been drawn by a magnet. "Salt-Hoss just told you. We're taking Jim Bowie's knife."

"You do just what Miss Belle tells you, *Cuchilo*," the old-timer advised, keeping his Henry rifle lined on the Ysabel Kid. "I don't want to see you get hurt, but that won't stop me happen I have to. I'm getting a mite too old for out-running posses and that old toad-sticker'll bring enough money to set me up comfortable some place."

"You'll never get away with it," Belle Boyd warned, speaking to Salt-Hoss as she looked straight at the lady outlaw and kept perfectly still. "I don't think she's told you who I really am."

"We'll take our chances for all of that," Starr declared, before the old-timer could make any comment. "So you start doing what I told you, Kid. You know I'm not bluffing."

"If I might make a suggestion, Miss Beauregard," Guillemot put in, having come to a halt as he had been requested. "You appear to have the upper hand, so I will make you a liberal offer for the knife and, of course, the pleasure of your company as far as Texas where we can close our deal."

"Am I in on that, *partner?*" the Kid inquired, without offering to comply with the girl's order.

"Hardly, under the circumstances," the Ox replied. "I will, of course, reimburse you for your services—always assuming that Miss Beauregard intends to leave you alive."

"If they'll let me, I do," Starr stated. "I'll leave your horses a couple of miles away, Kid. If two old hands like us can't get away with that much of a head start, we deserve to get caught."

"*Two*, Miss Beauregard?" Guillemot asked. "Do I take it that you are not going to accept my offer?"

"You might say that," Starr admitted.

"I don't think that Mr. Turtle will be kindly disposed towards you if I am compelled to complain about your actions," the Ox warned.

"He won't give a damn if you do," Starr corrected cheerfully, glancing at the left side window as the horses in the corral began to snort and move restlessly. "Your friends in New York riled him when they said 'You will' instead of 'Will you?' when they passed the word that you needed help. Kid, I'm getting awful tired of waiting for you to do what I said. And you stand *real* still, Belle Boyd!"

"*Belle Boyd!*" Guillemot repeated, staring at the slender girl. "Then you're not—"

"She's no more 'Betty Hardin' than I'm 'Magnolia Beauregard,'" Starr replied, deriving pleasure at the startled and baffled expression which came to the fat man's face after the superior and condescending way in which he had treated her ever since they had met.

"That's true, Mr. Guillemot," the Rebel Spy agreed. "And, seeing that introductions are in order," Miss Beauregard' is better known as Belle Starr.

"You asked Ram Turtle for the best help he could give,"

Starr pointed out, then her voice hardened. "Time's wasting, Kid. Start doing what—"

"You'll never get away with it, Starr," Boyd cautioned, watching for some way in which the hold upon them might be broken. "If Lon doesn't get you, I will. And I've got the whole of the United States Secret Service to back me in it."

"Hell's fire!" Salt-Hoss ejaculated. "You didn't say we'd be up against anything like *this*, Miss Belle—"

"What's spooking the horses?" the Kid interrupted, for the animals were still displaying evidence that something was disturbing them.

"Best take a look, Salt-Hoss," Starr ordered. "And don't you worry, we'll pull through like I promised."

Without taking his Henry out of alignment, the old-timer started to move in a crab-like fashion towards the window. Looking through it over his shoulder, he stiffened and tried to turn, yelling, "Hell, it's Ya—"

A shot crashed from outside the house, before Salt-Hoss could either finish his warning or complete the turn. Passing through his right temple, a bullet shattered out at the right in a hideous spray of bone splinters, brains and blood. Pitched across the room, he went down.

Springing forward, the Kid reached the window with his Winchester held ready for instant use, which was fortunate. He saw several stocky, thickset young Indian braves rushing towards the building. Their black hair was held back by headbands, but without decoration by feathers. Dressed in breechclouts and a variety of garments, they were armed with bow and arrows, or muzzle-loading and antiquated firearms. Lining his rifle, the Kid fired. Working the lever as one of the warriors fell, he changed his point of aim and tumbled another. Then Starr was at his side and her carbine dropped a third as he was raising his bow.

Putting aside her anger over Starr's attempted theft of the knife, Boyd darted forward. As the lady outlaw was running towards the Kid she snatched up the Henry which Salt-Hoss had dropped. With the weapon in her hands, she went to the door of the back room. Nor did she arrive a moment too soon. Several young Yaqui brave-hearts were approaching. Swinging up the rifle, she drove a bullet into the head of one of the attackers and was throwing the lever through its reloading cycle when the barrel of another weapon was thrust by her and roared to send a second brave to the Land of the Good Hunting.

Showing surprising speed for one of his bulk and normally lethargic movements, Guillemot had bent and snatched up his Sharps "Old Reliable" buffalo gun. After glancing out of the right side window to make sure that no danger was threatening from that direction, he had lumbered rapidly to join the Rebel Spy and take his part in the fighting.

Realizing that the Ox was armed with a single-shot rifle, Boyd thrust the Henry towards him. She opened her mouth to speak, but found that an explanation was unnecessary. Taking his left hand from the foregrip of the Sharps, he accepted the repeater. Then, paying no attention to Silk's body—having seen more than one corpse during her eventful young life— she ran to where the secretary had placed her saddle and slipped the Winchester carbine from its boot. However, by the time she had crossed to the window, and Guillemot—who had leaned his Sharps against the wall and moved forward—joined her, the Yaquis were running back up the slope.

"Are they pulling out, Belle?" the Kid called from the other room.

"Yes, up the slope at any rate," the Rebel Spy answered. "We dropped two, though."

"Can we come in and join you, Mr. Ysabel?" Guillemot requested.

"Should be all right," the Kid replied. "Only stop at the door so that you can keep an eye on them."

Backing from the room, Boyd and Guillemot looked at the remaining members of their party. Much to their surprise, they found that the Kid had rested his rifle against the wall, removed his hat and was unfastening his bandana. Starr had turned and was starring at the old-timer's body.

"Poor old Salt-Hoss," the lady outlaw sighed, raising her eyes to Boyd and showing genuine sorrow. "All he wanted was to get enough money to buy a spread somewhere that he wasn't known as an outlaw."

"May I ask what you're doing, Mr. Ysabel?" Guillemot inquired, watching the Kid dropping the bandana into the crown of his hat and starting to unbutton his shirt.

"Hey, *gringos!*" called a voice in Spanish. "Hey, *gringos.* Do any of you speak Mexican?"

"I do, *Manos Grande,*" the Kid replied, drawing off his shirt.

"You know my name?" the speaker yelled and there was surprise in his voice.

"My medicine told me you'd be coming," the Kid answered, freeing the pigging thong which connected the tip of the Dragoon's holster to his right thigh. He lowered his voice, looking at Boyd and addressing her in English. "Get the knife from my war bag and—"

"No white man has medicine," *Manos Grande* interrupted, before the rest of the instructions could be given.

"I'm a man of two people, like you," the Kid explained in Spanish, then reverted to English while unbuckling his gunbelt. "And the moccasins and my rifle's medicine boot."

"Yo!" Boyd responded, not knowing why the request had been made but setting off to carry it out.

"What are you—?" Guillemot commenced, staring in amazement as the young Texan laid his gunbelt on the floor by the hat and shirt.

"What tribe do you belong to?" *Manos Grande* demanded.

"The *Nemenuh,*" the Kid explained, starting to lever off his left boot. "Or, as others call us, the *Tshaoh.*"

"Just what is going—?" Guillemot tried again.

"I'd leave him to it, whatever it is," Starr advised, guessing what the Kid had in mind and knowing just how dangerous it would be. "He's trying to save our lives."

"Are you of the Enemy People?" *Manos Grande* wanted to know, translating the word *"Tshaoh."*

"My grandfather is Chief Long Walker of the Quick-Stingers," the Kid stated with pride. "My man-name is *Cuchilo.* I have taken and have never broken the oath of the *Pehnane* Dog Soldiers' war lodge."

"Does your medicine tell you why I have come, *Cuchilo?*" the Yaqui leader challenged.

"You have brought your men to be killed *trying* to take the big knife from me," the Kid answered, selecting his words with deliberate care and completing the removal of his boots.

"Not to try!" *Manos Grande* corrected. "I'm going to take it."

"Are these what you wanted, Lon?" Boyd inquired, bringing the knife, a pair of moccasins and a long pouch made of fringed bucksin and decorated with red, yellow and blue patterning.

"Sure," the Kid agreed and unfastened his waist belt. While opening his trousers' fly buttons, he replied to the Yaqui. "You'll lose many men before you even get near the house. Every one of us has a repeating rifle and many bullets. Don Arsenio gave me the knife—"

"And I am going to take it, then lead the *Ventoso* Yaqui to drive the old one from our lands," *Manos Grande* announced. "If you give it to me, I will let you ride away."

"You can't do it!" Guillemot protested in alarm, as the Kid removed his trousers and socks to stand clad only in the traditional blue breech-clout of a Comanche which he always wore instead of underpants. "Why not let him have *your* knife?"

If the Ox's suggestion was caused by seeing Starr bending to slide the Kid's weapon from its sheath and thinking that she had the same idea, he was rapidly disillusioned.

"He'd know what we'd done as soon as he touched the handle," the lady outlaw pointed out. "Leave it to Lon, he knows what he's doing."

"Well, *Cuchilo?*" *Manos Grande* bellowed impatiently. "Will you bring it to me, or do I come and fetch it?"

"Got you, you son-of-a-bitch!" the Kid enthused quietly yet vehemently and in English as he donned the moccasins. Resuming the use of Spanish and speaking louder, he went on, "Dare *you* come and fetch it, *Manos Grande?*" While speaking, he draped the *Pehnane* medicine pouch over his bare left shoulder and accepted the knives from the girls, his left hand shaking the sheath from Bowie's blade. "Not your brave-hearts, just *you* yourself."

"What are you trying to do?" Guillemot demanded.

"He's counting on making strong medicine with the knife," the Kid explained. "And if he doesn't get it, then he's through. So I'm betting he'll take up my challenge. Fact being, he'll have to."

"Then why not shoot him as he comes?" the Ox suggested.

"If you do, we'll never get out of here alive," Starr warned angrily. "I've told you that Lon knows what he's doing."

"Happen things go wrong," the Kid drawled, strolling to the front door, "save a bullet for yourselves."

"Count on it," Starr promised grimly. "Good luck, Lon. I'm sorry I tried to take the knife."

"You will be, if we come through," Boyd assured the lady outlaw. "Take care, Lon."

"I'll do my damnedest to," the Kid declared. "Let's hope there's a few old hands along with him."

"What did he mean?" Guillemot inquired, after the young Texan had left.

"If there're older warriors, they'll be more inclined to accept that *Manos Grande*'s medicine was bad if he fails and will take the party away," Starr explained and managed a weak grin at Boyd. "I might even take you up on it, if we come through."

Strolling out of the house in an apparently unconcerned fashion, the Kid made his way towards the edge of the chasm. However, as he was walking, he kept his eyes open and was alert for treachery. The Yaquis were moving into sight on the rim, but did not offer to advance towards the building. Instead, all were looking expectantly at one of their number; a well-built young warrior astride a big paint stallion and with a rifle cradled across his arm.

Coming to a halt facing the Indians, the Kid took the medicine pouch from his shoulder without relinquishing his hold on his weapon. Then he raised it and Bowie's knife into the air so that both could be seen.

"Here!" the Kid yelled. "I offer you the big knife—if you can come and take it. Or is *Manos Grande* like a woman who waits while the brave-hearts do the fighting and bring home the trophies for her to take?"

From his first sight of the attackers, the Kid had suspected that they were *Ventoso* Yaquis and had guessed what they were after. One of their people who worked on the *hacienda* must have taken them news of Serrano's gift to the Kid. So *Manos Grande* was taking the opportunity to gain possession of the big knife, which he alone could use one-handed, that had previously been unobtainable as it was kept in the well-defended house.

The words which the Kid had just spoken were a direct and deliberate challenge, one that no self-respecting warrior could ignore; particularly if he had asperations towards leading the other brave-hearts of his people into battle.

There was one danger. As the Kid had discovered while talking about the Indians with the *vaqueros* on the last afternoon at *Casa* Serrano, *Manos Grande*'s mother had been a Mexican *peon*. So he might not respond to the challenge in the fashion of a pure-blooded Yaqui. However, the Kid was gambling that he would. A man who was trying to live down what he regarded as the stigma of mixed parentage, which was how the *vaqueros* had described *Manos Grande*, was likely to be determined to uphold his people's traditions and beliefs rather than to go against them.

Sure enough, the warrior on the paint was handing his rifle to the grey-haired man who was nearest to him. Then he passed over his powder horn and ammunition bag. Peeling off the buckskin vest which he was wearing, he dropped it. Having done so, he set his horse into motion. None of the other braves offered to follow him, the Kid noted with relief. If the worst should happen, Guillemot and the girls would at least have an opportunity to sell their lives dearly.

"It's working!" Starr breathed, having watched what was happening.

"Surely if we shot him, the rest—" Guillemot began, but the words trailed into nothing as the girls glared furiously at him.

"If you even try, we'll shoot you in *both* arms so that you'll be alive when they get you!" Starr threatened. "Our only hope is that the Kid comes through."

Satisfied that all was going as well as could be expected, the Kid tossed Bowie's knife about thirty feet in the approaching rider's direction. Then he laid the medicine pouch on the ground at his feet and stood waiting for *Manos Grande* to arrive.

Letting his mount increase its pace, the Yaqui studied the tall, lean figure. He was not fooled by the relaxed-appearing way in which the *Tshaoh*—for that was how he now thought of the Kid—was standing, knowing that he was alert, watchful and ready to meet any eventuality. What was more, to have earned the man-name *"Cuchilo"* implied that he had attained considerable efficiency in and acclaim for wielding a knife in combat; no mean feat that, among the very capable ranks of the *Pehnane* Comanches' Dog Soldier war lodge.

Noticing the shape and dimensions of the weapon which the Kid was holding, *Manos Grande* frowned and stirred uneasily on his horse's back. He wondered if he was being tricked. The knife on the ground might not be the same that had excited his envy at *Casa* Serrano and upon which he was basing his hopes for the future. It looked as if it was, but he was too far away to be certain.

What was more, being so much alike, perhaps the *Tshaoh*'s knife possessed similar magical properties. That was a sobering and disturbing thought. However, *Manos Grande* knew that he could not turn back without a complete loss of face. He had many enemies, including a few who had joined his raiding party.. If he should return without the knife, even if his sole intention was to collect and use his rifle as a means of dealing with the *Tshaoh,* they would claim that his medicine was bad and leave him.

Accepting that he had no other course except to go on, *Manos Grande* gave thought as to how to deal with his enemy. He discarded the idea of using the knife which hung sheathed on his belt. If the *Tshaoh*'s weapon was made from the same kind of steel as the one from *Casa* Serrano, it would be capable of breaking his own blade.

With that in mind, *Manos Grande* urged his paint to a faster pace. It would never do for his rivals, or the waiting man, to think that he was suffering from doubts and uncertainties. Quitting the fast-moving animal's back, he alighted with a cat-like agility. Advancing on foot, he reached for the knife. The moment his right hand—which was unusually large for his stature, hence his man-name—closed on the hilt, he knew it was the weapon which he required as a means of becoming the war leader who would guide his people to victory over the Mexicans.

Watching the Yaqui pick up the knife, the Kid noticed that he did not grasp it in the usual Indian fashion. Instead of the blade extending from the bottom of the hand—which allowed

only two types of blow, a downwards chop at the side of the
neck and a horizontal hacking slash—it protruded ahead of his
thumb and forefinger. The Kid held his own weapon in the
same manner.

Coming closer, *Manos Grande* showed how—for all his
hatred of the Mexican side of his blood—he was not averse
to adopting that nation's methods of knife-fighting.

Moving lightly on spread-apart feet and well-flexed knees,
their torsos inclined forward so as to offer a smaller target,
each man kept his right arm bent and the knife at hip level. He
held his left hand extended slightly to one side as an aid to
retaining his balance and to help with his protection from his
enemy's weapon.

Circling for a few seconds, watching each other's eyes for
any hint of what action was being considered, the Kid and
Manos Grande were like two great cats. However, the Texan
was in no hurry to start. Time was on his side, to a certain
degree, as he did not have a reason for preventing his companions from thinking that he was afraid to make an attack.

While aware of the urgency and the inadvisability of de-
laying from taking the offensive, *Manos Grande* was unwilling
to allow it to drive him into being rash. The knife was very
heavy and, despite its excellent balance, seemed somewhat
awkward after the weapon to which he had become accustomed.
So he would be worse than foolish if he was to take chances
with such an obviously competent enemy.

Guessing what was causing *Manos Grande* to act in such
a cautious manner, the Kid feinted a cut towards his forward
knee. Out thrust the Yaqui's left hand in an attempt to either
grasp or deflect the Texan's knife arm. Like a flash, the Kid
changed the direction that his blade was taking and he succeeded in opening a narrow, shallow gash on the other man's
left forearm.

Manos Grande could not restrain a low hiss of surprise and
pain, but he realized that the injury was only minor and would
not incapacitate him. So he responded swiftly with a backhand
swing at the Kid's head. Although the Texan had no wish to
allow his own blade to meet the Yaqui's in an edge to edge
clash, he reacted before he could stop himself. Just in time,
he contrived to parry the attack with the flat of the blade.

Recoiling a long pace, the Kid saw that *Manos Grande*'s right arm was exposed. However, the cut at it which he launched failed to connect due to the speed with which the Yaqui withdrew. In doing so, *Manos Grande* straightened his torso. Unfortunately, by the time that the Kid had recovered his own balance, *Manos Grande* was once more in the "on guard" position.

Once again, the two men circled each other. Watched by the girls and Guillemot—who had left the door from where he had been keeping the Yaquis on the rim under observation—and the men who had joined *Manos Grande* on the raid, the fighting pair decided upon their next moves.

"Your medicine is bad, *Manos Grande*," the Kid mocked as he avoided a raking slash aimed at his chest.

Goaded to recklessness by the taunt, the Yaqui attempted an uppercut. However, although the Kid twisted rearwards at the waist, he did not attempt to counter the blow. Instead, he bounded aside and crouched low, using his left hand on the ground for support. At the same moment, he made a swing as if trying to rip open his enemy's forward leg. Whirling his own knife downwards and to the left in an attempt to parry the blow, *Manos Grande* discovered just a fraction too late that it had been another feint and not a serious attack.

Straightening up, the Kid changed the direction in which his weapon was travelling. As it flashed to the left, his greater reach and the extra half inch's advantage offered by his knife over Bowie's blade proved their worth. Although *Manos Grande* tried to move clear, he failed to go quite far enough and he received a raking gash across the forehead.

For all the pain which the wound must have caused him, the Yaqui responded with some speed. His own knife was pointing towards the ground and to his left, but he reversed its course. Seeing the concave swoop of the false edge rising in his direction and being aware that it was just as sharp and deadly as the main cutting edge, the Kid twisted to the left and clear. Still displaying the same rapidity of movement, *Manos Grande* pivoted into a kick. The ball of his foot caught the Kid in the small of the back with considerable force, propelling him towards the chasm.

Only by an effort did the Kid manage to bring himself to

a halt. Even then, he was teetering on the very edge of the sheer wall which dropped almost a thousand feet to the raging rapids of the *Rio de la Babia*. However, in his struggle to regain his equilibrium, he released his knife and it fell a short distance away.

Despite the blood which was running from the wound on his forehead and into his eyes, *Manos Grande* could see that his enemy was disarmed. Letting out a wild victory whoop, he charged and thrust forward with his weapon. By that time, however, the Kid was in full control of his movements. Weaving aside, he caught the Yaqui's knife-wrist in both hands and, pivoting, heaved. As *Manos Grande* was rung by him, he released his hold. Unable to stop, the Yaqui went over the edge—and took James Bowie's knife along with him.

Moving forward, the Kid watched *Manos Grande* plunging downwards. There was a tiny splash which might have been caused by the knife, having slipped from his hand, falling into the torrent. It was obscured as he arrived and was instantly swirled along by the racing current. There was over half a mile of violent rapids, speckled with jagged and sharp-pointed rocks. Not that *Manos Grande* knew much of them. He was dead before he had gone a hundred yards.

Turning away, the Kid saw the other Yaquis talking among themselves on the rim, after which they swung their horses around and rode away. Sucking his breath in, the young Texan gathered up his knife and medicine boot. Then he walked slowly towards the house. The girls and Guillemot came out to meet him.

"We don't need to worry about anybody else trying to steal old Jim Bowie's knife any more," the Kid told them *"Manos Grande* took it over the edge with him."

CHAPTER SIXTEEN

This Time I Can Really Fight!

"I've been looking forward to this ever since I caught you pretending to the Bad Bunch that you were me," Belle Starr remarked in a matter-of-fact manner which gave no indication of her intentions, then swung her left fist across to catch the right side of the Rebel Spy's jaw.

The blow sent Belle Boyd reeling several steps, but she did not go down. Catching her balance, she weaved aside just in time to avoid Starr's follow-up attack. As the lady outlaw blundered by, unable to stop herself, Boyd drove an elbow hard into her back and brought an involuntary squeak of pain.

Although Octavius Xavier Guillemot had been angry over the loss of James Bowie's knife, he had grudgingly conceded that the Ysabel Kid could hardly be blamed for how it had come about. There had been little discussion on the matter, however, as the Kid had warned that they might still be in danger from the Yaquis. The death of their leader had caused them to withdraw, but some other warrior might assumed command and wish to test his medicine by trying to avenge the braves who had been killed.

Going back into the house, the girls, the Kid and Guillemot had made ready to continue the defense. The need to do so had not arisen. Just before dark, a party of Don Arsenio Serrano's *vaqueros* had arrived. Word of *Manos Grande*'s intentions had reached their *patrón* and he had sent them to help deal with the Yaquis. On learning of the fight, the *vaqueros* had commiserated with the Kid and agreed with him that the knife was beyond any hope of recovery.

Having spent the night with the party, after breakfast that morning the *vaqueros* had helped move the buckboard and horses across the *Rio de la Babia*. However, their offer to help bury Anthony Silk and Salt-Hoss had been refused by the Kid. He had claimed that Guillemot was so filled with remorse over their deaths that he wished to dig the graves himself. On the Ox starting to object, the Kid had remarked pointedly that it was a *very* long *walk* to the nearest town. Looking at the grim expression on the Indian-dark young face, Guillemot had known that he was not listening to an idle threat and had done the Kid's bidding.

There had been no mention of Starr's attempted theft of the knife the previous evening. When the Kid had raised the matter with Boyd that morning, she had said that she would attend to it.

After the *vaqueros* had departed, Boyd had suggested that— like a drowning man was said to clutch at a straw—*Manos Grande* might have clung to the knife and, if so, they could perhaps find it with his body downstream from the chasm. Although none of them had believed it was likely, the Kid had offered to make a search. Guillemot had agreed to accompany him, but Boyd had said that she and Starr would wait with the horses. The lady outlaw had not raised any objections, much to the Ox's surprise.

Once the two men had ridden out of sight, Starr and Boyd had secured the horses and went to the sandy edge of the river. As the lady outlaw had guessed what the Rebel Spy had in mind, she had taken the offensive.

Rubbing at her back as she swung around, Starr walked straight into a jab from Boyd's right fist. Its knuckles caught her on the nose, hard enough to sting and make her eyes water even though it was almost at the end of its flight. Pivoting like a ballet dancer, Boyd demonstrated the skill at *savate*—French foot boxing—which had served her so well on numerous occasions. Like the lady outlaw, she had donned a pair of moccasins that morning. For all that, the kick which thudded against Starr's ribs was hard enough to send the heavier girl staggering. While she gasped, she retained her upright posture.

"The thing is," Boyd commented, gliding forward as the other girl came to a halt, "this time I can really fight."

"So can I!" Starr warned, lowering her head and charging with hands reaching to take hold.

On the occasion to which the lady outlaw referred, although they had tangled, neither had been able to display her true ability in fighting.[1] Both had frequently wondered what the result would have been if they had, and so were not averse to finding out.

Instead of allowing the lady outlaw to come into contact with her, Boyd leapt into the air. Her hands slapped on to the brunette head as she leap-frogged over. Letting out an angry squeak, Starr turned. Boyd had twirled around on landing. Once again she bounded into the air, using the technique which would become known in wrestling as a drop-kick. Seeing her danger, Starr jumped backwards. Boyd's feet caught the other girl's full bosom, but once again were just too far away to arrive with their full impact. However, gasping in pain, Starr was forced to continue her retreat.

Rebounding, Boyd landed rump first on the sand. Flinging herself forward, Starr meant to land on the other girl and make the most of her weight advantage. Tilting over so that she once again avoided Starr's hands, Boyd brought her feet under the lady outlaw's body and thrust upwards. Turning half a somersault, Starr landed supine. The soft sand broke her fall and, expecting to be attacked, she rolled rapidly on to her face. From there, she forced herself on to her hands and knees. While doing so, she found out why her expectation had not been fulfilled.

Finding that the skirt was impeding her agility, which would

1. Told in: *The Bad Bunch*.

be needed to offset Starr's extra pounds of weight, Boyd freed her skirt as soon as she had bounded up from foot-rolling the other girl. It was sliding down, revealing that she was wearing her riding breeches, as Starr dived at her. The brunette head rammed into Boyd's mid-section, then Starr's arms locked around her waist and bore her to the ground.

At first female instincts sent Boyd's fingers into Starr's brunette locks, taking a healthy hold and tearing at them as she was crushed against the sand. On releasing the Rebel Spy's waist and duplicating her actions, Starr found that the boyishly short black hair offered a far less effective grasp for pulling upon. Bracing herself, as the torment she was inflicting caused Starr to writhe in agony, Boyd managed to roll her from the top. Boyd hoped to be able to escape and rise, having no desire to fight at such close quarters as doing so would favor the other girl. As she released the hair and tried to get up, Starr gave a heave which toppled her over and regained the upper position. Straddling the Rebel Spy's slender waist and kneeling over her, Starr started to rain slaps at her face.

With her head rocking from side to side as the blows landed, Boyd wriggled and squirmed with furious desperation. Fortunately for her, Starr had not been able to trap her arms. After making a few abortive attempts to grab the brunette's wrists, Boyd acted in a more effective manner. Scooping up a handful of sand, she flung it into the other girl's face. Then, while Starr was still half blinded, she surged her body upwards like a bow. Although the lady outlaw was pitched from her perch, Boyd did not resume the fight on the ground. Instead, she rolled free and, with her cheeks reddened by the slaps, jumped to her feet.

Staying clear until Starr was also up, Boyd moved into the attack. Clenching her fists, the lady outlaw advanced to meet her. The fight went on for another half an hour. Some of the time, they used their fists like a couple of men. In between, they wrestled in feminine fashion. There were occasions, such as when Starr held her head in chancery and pummelled at her face with the other hand, that Boyd came close to regretting the decision to inflict summary punishment for the attempted theft of Bowie's knife. However, the Rebel Spy managed to escape and launched a swift-moving *savate* attack which more than repaid what she had received.

Starr had been in more than one rough-house, but not even Calamity Jane had proved to be as tough as the Rebel Spy. There were muscles which felt like steel springs in Boyd's slender arms and legs. Not only was she extremely competent at *savate*, which made use of punching as well as kicking, but she showed that she could hold her own when it came to old-fashioned knock-down-and-drag-out brawling.

Gradually Boyd began to gain the upper hand. Her speed and knowledge of *savate* slowly swung the balance of the scales in her favor. To the dazed, exhausted and suffering Starr, it seemed that every other second a bony fist was impacting against her face, naked breasts—the brawling had left both of them clad in nothing but their breeches—and stomach. They were punctuated by the kicks which the Rebel Spy seemed to be able to launch from any angle and as high as her head. Starr might have felt grateful that Boyd had not been wearing riding boots, for the results with her bare feet were sufficiently painful.

Staggering on wobbly legs, the girls were trading exhausted punches and slaps. At last, making a final desperate attempt to get her hands on Boyd, Starr found they flopped limply to her sides and her knees began to buckle. She made a despairing effort to carry on, stumbling forward with her mouth trailing open and bosom heaving as she tried to drag air into her tortured lungs.

The sight gave an almost equally spent Boyd the fillip that she needed. Summoning every last dreg of energy that she could muster, she put all her rapidly failing strength behind a roundhouse swing with her left fist. Obligingly, if inadvertantly, Starr reeled into range. Caught alongside the jaw, she spun around and crashed face down on to the sand. A moment later, Boyd collapsed on top of her.

"Good heavens!" Guillemot ejaculated, staring at the two girls as he was climbing laboriously from the largest of the harness horses which he had been riding. "Have you been fighting?"

There was good cause for the Ox's comment. Almost ninety

minutes had elapsed since Boyd had delivered the *coupe de grace* to Starr. Recovering first, the Rebel Spy had dragged her beaten opponent into the water and revived her. After having ascertained that the lady outlaw had had enough, Boyd had suggested they should try to make themselves look more presentable before the men returned. Although they had washed away the sand which perspiration had caused to adhere to them, done the best they could to alter the tangled messes in which their hair had been left, stopped the bleeding from noses and lips, and changed into fresh clothing, their bruised faces left little doubt as to what they had been doing.

"It seemed like a good idea at the time," Starr answered, speaking somewhat thickly, and touched her jaw with a delicate finger. "Now I'm not so sure."

"Who won?" the Kid asked with a grin, having suspected what might happen when he had accepted Boyd's suggestion and taken Guillemot in search of the knife.

"Boyd got lucky," Starr explained, throwing a wry grin at the Rebel Spy.

"Sore loser," Boyd sniffed, but with no greater show of animosity. "Did you have any luck, Lon?"

"Nope," the Kid replied. Having dismounted, he jerked a thumb towards the fat man. "Mr. Guillemot allows that we can't put him in the hoosegow for what he's done."

"I doubt whether you could," the Ox declared. "And more to the point, as I have not committed any crime—no matter what my intentions might have been—I'm sure that, in view of my past and, possibly, future services to them, I don't think Miss Boyd's organization would want me to be incarcerated."

"You could be right," the Rebel Spy conceded. "But you might have notions about getting revenge on us—"

"Perish the thought, dear lady," Guillemot boomed. "Much as the loss of Bowie's knife rankles, I wouldn't think of wasting time, money and effort on idle revenge—"

"Particularly when trying to do it might mean that word would get out how the Ox was fooled by a girl and a Texas cowhand," Starr continued. "It'd make him the laughing stock throughout the criminal world."

Watching Guillemot's face, the Kid saw anger flicker briefly across it to be replaced by grudging admiration.

"By gad!" the Ox boomed, slapping a fat thigh with the palm of his hand. "By gad! And to think that I expected to be dealing with dull-witted rubes! I must be getting old." Then he ran his appreciative gaze over the three young people and went on, "I don't suppose you would care to accompany me to Europe and assist me in a venture which had interested me for several years. One which, if it is successful, will be at least as profitable as the sale of Bowie's secret."

"What'd that be?" the Kid inquired.

"Locating and acquiring a statuette of a falcon, sir," Guillemot replied. "It is made of solid gold and encrusted with the finest jewels to be looted from the Crusades.[2] Its value, sir, in the right circles, is immense."

"Sounds like it might be," the Kid drawled.

"Then you'll accompany me?" the Ox asked.

"I don't reckon so," the Kid replied. "I'm not saying's I don't reckon you'd play fair, even if I don't, but I'd sooner stay on my own range."

"And work as a forty-dollars-a-month cowhand?" Guillemot challenged.

"Why not?" the Kid countered. "'Ole Devil's a damned good boss and Betty Hardin's nothing like Belle pretended. You might not believe me, but even after you'd told me about Bowie's knife, I'd still have taken it back for his kin."

"I *do* believe you," Guillemot stated and there was respect in his voice. "How about you, ladies?"

"I'm satisfied with what I am," Boyd replied. "Why don't you go, Belle?"

"Like Lon says, I'd sooner stay on my own range," Starr answered.

"Tell you what, sir," the Kid drawled. "Just to show there's no hard feelings, on the way back to San Antonio, I'll show you some mighty fine hunting."

"You may as well, sir," Guillemot boomed enthusiastically. "I might as well get *something* out of the quest for Bowie's blade. And to show *you* that there are no ill-feelings on my part, I'll give you the clasp-knife which James Black made."

---

2. Full details of the statuette can be found in Dashiell Hammett's *The Maltese Falcon*.

Appendix One

During the War Between The States at seventeen years of age, Dustine Edward Marsden Fog had won promotion in the field and was put in command of the Texas Light Cavalry's hard-riding, harder-fighting Company "C".[1] Leading them in the Arkansas Campaign, he had earned the reputation for being an exceptionally capable military raider the equal of the South's other exponents, John Singleton Mosby and Turner Ashby.[2] In addition to preventing a pair of Union fanatics from starting an Indian uprising which would have decimated most of Texas,[3] he had supported Belle Boyd, the Rebel Spy,[4] on two of her most dangerous missions.[5]

1. Told in *You're in Command Now, Mr. Fog*.
2. Told in: *The Big Gun; Under the Stars and Bars; The Fastest Gun in Texas* and *Kill Dusty Fog*.
3. Told in: *The Devil Gun*.
4. Further details of Belle Boyd's career are given in: *The Hooded Riders; The Bad Bunch; To Arms, To Arms in Dixie; The South Will Rise Again* and *The Whip and the War Lance*.
5. Told in: *The Colt and the Saber* and *The Rebel Spy*.

When the War had finished, he had become the segundo of the great OD Connected ranch in Rio Hondo County, Texas. Its owner and his uncle, General Ole Devil Hardin, had been crippled in a riding accident[6] and it had thrown much of the work—including handling an important mission upon which the good relations between the United States and Mexico had hung in the balance[7]—upon him. After helping to gather horses and replenish the ranch's depleted remuda,[8] he had been sent to assist Colonel Charles Goodnight on the trail drive to Fort Sumner which had done much to help the Lone Star State to recover from the impoverished conditions left by the war.[9] With that achieved, he had been equally successful in helping Goodnight to prove that it would be possible to take herds of cattle to the railroad in Kansas.[10]

Having proven himself to be a first class cowhand, Dusty went on to be acknowledged as a very capable trail boss,[11] round up captain,[12] and a town-taming lawman.[13] In a contest at the Cochise County Fair, he won the title of the Fastest Gun In The West, by beating many other exponents of the *pistolero* arts.[14]

Dusty Fog never found his lack of stature an impediment. In addition to being naturally strong, he had taught himself to be completely ambidextrous. Possessing fast reflexes, he could draw and fire either, or both, of his Colts with lightning speed and great accuracy. Ole Devil Hardin's valet, Tommy Okasi, was Japanese and from him Dusty had learned *ju jitsu* and *karate*. Neither had received much publicity in the Western world, so the knowledge was very useful when he had to fight bare-handed against larger, heavier and stronger men.

6. Told in: *"The Paint"* episode of: *The Fastest Gun in Texas*.
7. Told in: *The Ysabel Kid*.
8. Told in: *.44 Caliber Man* and *A Horse Called Mogollon*.
9. Told in: *Goodnight's Dream* and *From Hide and Horn*.
10. Told in: *Set Texas Back on Her Feet*.
11. Told in: *Trail Boss*.
12. Told in: *The Man From Texas*.
13. Told in: *Quiet Town; The Making of a Lawman; The Trouble Busters; The Small Texan* and *The Town Tamers*.
14. Told in: *Gun Wizard*.

Appendix Two

The only daughter of Long Walker, war leader of the Pehnane—Wasp, Quick Stinger, or Raider—Comanche Dog Soldier lodge and his French Creole *pairaivo*[1] married an Irish
Kentuckian adventurer called Sam Ysabel, but died giving birth
to their first child. Given the name Loncey Dalton Ysabel, the
boy was raised in the fashion of the *Nemenuh*.[2] With his father
away much of the time on the family business of first mus-
tanging, then smuggling, his education had been left to his
maternal grandfather.[3] From Long Walker, he had learned all
those things a Comanche warrior must know; how to ride the
wildest, freshly caught mustang, or when raiding—a polite
name for the favorite *Nemenuh* sport of horsestealing—to sub-
jugate a domesticated mount to his will; to follow the faintest
of tracks and conceal traces of his own passing; to locate hidden

1. *Pairaivo:* first, or favorite, wife.
2. *Nemenuh:* "The People," the Comanche Indians' name for their nation.
3. Told in: *Comanche.*

enemies, yet remain concealed himself when the need arose; to move in silence through the thickest of cover or on the darkest of nights; and to be highly proficient in the use of a variety of weapons. In all these subjects, the boy had proved an excellent pupil. He had inherited his father's rifle-shooting skill and, while not real fast on the draw—taking slightly over a second, where a tophand would come close to half of that time—he could perform adequately with his colt Second Model Dragoon revolver. His excellent handling of one as a weapon had gained him the man-name *Cuchilo*, "the Knife" among the *Pehnane*.

Joining his father on smuggling trips along the Rio Grande, he had become known to the Mexicans of the border country as *Cabrito;* which had come from hearing white men referring to him as the Ysabel Kid. Smuggling did not attract mild-mannered, gentle-natured pacifists, but even the toughest and roughest men on the bloody border had learned that it did not pay to tangle with Sam Ysabel's son. His education and up-bringing had not been such that he was possessed of an over-inflated sense of the sanctity of human life. When crossed, he dealt with the situation like a *Pehnane* Dog Soldier—to which lodge of savage, efficient warriors he belonged—swiftly and in a deadly effective manner.

During the War, the Kid and his father had commenced by riding as scouts for the Grey Ghost, John Singleton Mosby. Later, their specialized talents had been used by having them collect and deliver to the Confederate States' authorities in Texas supplies which had been run through the U.S. Navy's blockade into Matamoros, or purchased elsewhere in Mexico. It had been hard, dangerous work and never more so than on the two occasions when they had been involved in missions with Belle Boyd.[4]

Sam Ysabel had been murdered soon after the end of the War. While hunting for the killers, the Kid had met Dusty Fog and, later, Mark Counter. Engaged on a mission of international importance, Dusty had been very grateful for the Kid's assistance. When it had been brought to a successful conclusion, learning that the Kid no longer wished to continue a career of

4. Told in: *The Bloody Border* and *Back to the Bloody Border*.

smuggling, Dusty had offered him work at the OD Connected ranch. When the Kid had stated that he knew little about being a cowhand, he had been told that it was his skill as a scout that would be required. His talents in that line had been most useful to the floating outfit.[5]

In fact, the Kid's acceptance had been of great benefit all round. Dusty had gained a loyal friend, ready to-stick by him through any danger. The ranch had obtained the services of an extremely capable and efficient man. For his part, the Kid had been turned from a life of petty crime—with the ever-present danger of having it develop into more serious law-breaking—and became a useful member of society. Peace officers and honest citizens might have been thankful for that as he would have made a terrible and murderous outlaw if he had been driven into such a life.

Obtaining his first repeating rifle while in Mexico with Dusty and Mark, the Kid became acknowledged as a master in its use. In fact, at the Cochise County Fair he won his first prize—one of the fabulous Winchester Models of 1873 "One Of A Thousand" rifles—against very stiff competition.[6] Also it was in a great part through his efforts that the majority of the Comanche Indian bands agreed to go on to the Reservation.[7] Nor could Dusty Fog have cleaned out the outlaw town of Hell without the Kid's assistance.[8]

5. Floating outfit: a group of four to six cowhands employed on a large ranch to work the more distant sections of the property. Taking food in a chuck wagon, or "greasy sack" on the back of a mule, they would be away from the ranch house for weeks at a time. Because of General Hardin's prominence in the affairs of Texas, the OD Connected's floating outfit were frequently sent to assist his friends who found themselves in trouble or danger.

6. Told in: _Gun Wizard._

7. Told in: _Sidewinder._

8. Told in: _Hell in the Palo Duro_ and _Go Back to Hell._

Appendix Three

Wanting a son and learning that his wife, Electra, could not have any more children, Vincent Charles Boyd had insisted that his only daughter, Belle,[1] be given thorough training in several subjects which were not normally regarded as being necessary for a wealthy Southron girl. At seventeen, she could ride a horse—astride or side-saddle—as well as any of her fox-hunting male neighbors; men who were to supply the South with its superlative cavalry. Not only that, but she was a skilled performer with a sword, an excellent shot with handgun or rifle, and expert in *savate,* French fist and foot boxing. All of which were to stand her in good stead in the future.

Shortly before the War Between The States had commenced a mob of pro-Union rabble had stormed the Boyd plantation. They had murdered her parents and wounded her, setting fire

1. According to American fictionist-genealogist Philip Jose Fraser's researches, Belle Boyd is related—the aunt of—to Jane Porter, who married Lord Greystoke, Tarzan of the Apes.

to her home before being driven off by the family's Negro servants. On her recovery, Belle had joined her cousin, Rose Greenhow, who was operating a spy ring. However, wanting to find the two leaders of the mob, who were serving with the Union's Secret Service she had taken the active and dangerous task of delivering her fellow agents' findings to the Confederate States' authorities. Gaining proficiency and acquiring the name, "the Rebel Spy," she had graduated to handling risky and important assignments. On two of them, she had been assisted by the already legendary Dusty Fog[2] and a third had brought her into contact with the equally famous young Texan called the Ysabel Kid.[3] However, her quest for the murderers of her parents did not come to its successful conclusion until shortly after the War had ended.[4]

On signing the oath of allegiance to the Union, Belle had been allowed to join the United States Secret Service. Despite her enmity for that organization during the War, she had served it loyally and with efficiency. She had been responsible for the breaking up of the notorious and deadly Bad Bunch,[5] assisted by lady outlaw Belle Starr and Martha "Calamity Jane" Canary.[6] Then she had brought to an end the activities of the Brotherhood For Southron Freedom, with the help of Ole Devil Hardin's floating outfit.[7] Her latest assignment, before becoming involved with Octavius Xavier Guillemot's attempt to gain possession of James Bowie's knife, had brought her together with Calamity Jane for a second time and they had contrived to prevent what might have developed into a war between the United States and Great Britain.[8]

While the Yankees might have had every reason to hate the Rebel Spy during the War, they had no cause to feel other than gratitude to her once it had ended.

2. Told in: *The Colt and the Saber* and *The Rebel Spy*.
3. Told in: *The Bloody Border*.
4. Told in: *Back to the Bloody Border*.
5. Told in: *The Bad Bunch*.
6. Details of Martha Jane Canary's career are given in the author's "Calamity Jane" series of books.
7. Told in: *To Arms! To Arms, in Dixie!* and *The South Will Rise Again*.
8. Told in: *The Whip and the War Lance*.

SONS OF TEXAS

**Book one in the exciting new saga
of America's Lone Star state!**

TOM EARLY

Texas, 1816. A golden land of
opportunity for anyone who dared
to stake a claim in its destiny...and
its dangers...

Filled with action, adventure,
drama and romance, *Sons of Texas*
is the magnificent epic story of
America in the making...the
people, places, and passions that
made our country great.

Look for each new book in the series!